MINUTEMEN

Nick May

Eucatastrophe Press
www.eucatastrophepress.com

2011

This is purely a work of fiction. All characters and
events (except for one particularly large oil spill) are
strictly products of the author's imagination.

Cover Design: Nick May
Illustrated by: Nick May

ISBN10: 1-893729-09-5
ISBN13: 978-1-893729-09-4
Library of Congress Control Number: 2011939117

Eucatastrophe Press
P. O. Box 841
Gonzalez, FL 32560

eucatastrophepress.com

To the Rockwells,
for everything that you are to me.

TABLE
OF
CONTENTS

Book I

THOM

I was sitting there thinking about all the sin that must have layered that filthy, modern pleather. How many people before me had sat there and done the same or worse? I bet if I had reached down in that crack, I would have found more than I bargained for. There were dudes across from me having drinks. A woman and her son stood at the bar. She let her boy stick the tip in himself. "Thanks," the chick said, as she piled on more whipped cream. It's a sick world, man. How many times was I going to find myself in there? Steam and steel; girls grinding this and that. Typical Tuesday night in the café at Box-Ear Book Store.

I shook my head in disgust as I returned to the spring issue of *Entrepreneur.* I hated that kind of crap, but it was what I had to be reading if she ever grew the balls to come over and say hello. Did I seriously just say that? Here I am: a twenty-something-year-old dude blaming girls for not having balls. That's like standing in front of a tree while pointing your finger at its trunk, saying, "Speak, you lame tree!" It's not in a poplar's nature to have a conversation—just like it's not in a woman's nature to be proactive. You can't fix science, man, no matter how hard you try. I heard a story once about a man who cursed a tree, causing it to wither instantaneously. That's what I was trying to do here—except in a different way that might have some passive wear on this girl's senses.

I wasn't being a stalker. I know when you hear that, you automatically assume it means: "check it out, so I'm stalking this girl, right?" but I'm serious. Some men are addicted to porn, and some just appreciate how a nude female is put together. All I'm saying is that dif-ferent people have different motives. Whatever—that's beside

1

the point. The chick in Box-Ear—she was by no means nude. She just worked down there, and I read (or pretended to read). I really did just like being down there. It was a cool place to hang out, despite the music—*Sounds of Soft-Core*, and the endless chatter of home schoolers on "field trips." It was situated near the beach in one of those high-class culture hubs where everyone wears Guy Harvey t-shirts. It was usually pretty crowded, but the oil had been keeping the masses to a minimum, too. The threat of tar-slathered beaches was enough to keep the tourists and spring-breakers away for at least a little while. I got stuff done if she didn't walk by too much. I wasn't being a stalker. I know when you hear that, you automatically ... whatever, I was stalking her. I'm telling you, though, there were old guys in there who were dangerously stalker-esque. Maybe it's not creepy if you're the same age. We had to be the same age.

I'd go down there some days and wouldn't see her at all. That helped me to feel like I wasn't there for the wrong reason, and it kept people from drawing conclusions. These said "people" drawing said "conclusions" were the same people who had no clue I was even alive, much less making plans for my next murder. Joking. I just wanted to ask her out or something. What does that even mean? "Hey, you wanna grab some coffee?" Screw coffee. I'd never done anything that reckless in my entire life. I was the guy who cultivated these lasting friendships with girls, and then, when the time was right, we did it—you know—made it official. Like Facebook official. In high school, you get four long years to make an impression. You get to invest in girls, even if it's for later. I had time to be funny, time to be charming. In the quote unquote real world, girls are terrifying. Most of them do pretty scary things. Most of them are way hotter than you're ready for, and the one's that aren't ... well, they date you for five years, get hot, people assume you're their little brother, she realizes she's hot and jets. It's a really cool situation.

I was there. I was constantly working out scenarios in my head where I walk up to her and say something incredibly brave—not like the douchers on the MTV beach with surefire lines like, "Hey ... beer?" I'd say something like, "listen, I know we don't know each other, but you're really distracting—can I take you to a movie?"

"You can't just go up to girls you don't know and say stuff like that," Memory would say. Not my memory—my friend, Memory. She was sort of my lab rat.

"Well, I'm not buying beer and taking it down there," I'd say. She'd laugh a little.

"You need to get to know her. Ask her what her name is and tell her something nice."

"Memory, that's garbage. No one likes or believes that," I'd say—looking for new rats.

"Well, that's what Kyle did with me." Kyle was a toolbag. She should have been dating me and taking my mind off this girl.

The key factor that always played out in my mind was the boyfriend. If a girl that looked like that didn't have a boyfriend, then I knew I could at least spend the next five or six months reminding her that the best guys come in dull packages. I didn't have a problem re-teaching a girl how to be a decent human being. I had a problem being like all the dudes who'd ever hit on my girlfriends in front of me—dudes whose last concern happened to be my existence.

"Hey, what's your name?" he'd ask her in the line at the grocery store. She'd smile and answer. I'd suddenly be sitting in the child seat of the buggy wondering what to be more pissed about—his question or her reaction. Maybe she left because she was tired of me not standing out.

"Hey, buddy, I'm not her little brother!" I'd think (and only think). "Man, and what if I was? That still doesn't justify your blatant disregard for me as a person!" Anyway, I had enough respect for the Man Code to at least understand that if and when I approached her, my first concern would be finding out if she had a boyfriend, and if so, I'm done, and the world ends up being an easier place for me to live in. Loyalty, son, even to men you don't know. That's a quality Beer Guy won't have. Ever.

It was now or never. Well, that's not exactly true. I could have done it whenever, but I figured she'd at least be alone back there in the Test Prep section, putting out books for GREs I'd never take. I got up from my oversized chair in the café and walked towards the bathroom. There was a home school kid sitting in the aisle with a fat, older guy. They were playing one of those card games that makes your penis smaller. I had to step over them. Hopefully one of them was her boyfriend. I could probably be more charming.

I skipped the bathroom and did a walk-by past the aisle she was working in. I got that hot heart sweat, not native to merely seeing nice features. She was wearing 552s and a white t-shirt. Her clothes fit. Why didn't all girls just understand the simple language that Levis spoke? She really wasn't the kind of girl I would

4

typically gawk over. She was attractive to me for a weird reason that I couldn't really explain. She was thin, man, almost dead. Short hair. Weird smile—but I was into it. I put the copy of *Entrepreneur* back on the shelf and walked right over. I was committed.

"Hey," I said.

"Hi," she replied sheepishly. Here we were.

"What's your name?" I asked.

"Dee," she said.

"Oh, that's different."

"Thanks …" she turned back to her work.

"No, I mean, that's just a cool name." We laughed a little as she faced me again.

"Can I help you with anything?" She asked. Yeah you dumb book jockey! How about this awkwardness?!

"This is going to sound forward," I started, "but um, do you have a boyfriend … perchance?" Respect.

"Um, No," she laughed. At least she was laughing. I didn't care that it was at me.

"Cool. Would it be alright if I gave you my phone number, and you can just call me or text me if you want," I said as I took out a piece of college ruled paper I had pre-torn and left blank with the intention of writing on. It was the kind of thing you just don't remember any part of when you walk away. I probably wrote it wrong. Probably wrote my social security number.

"Sure. Thanks," she said. Her voice was different than I had expected. It had a mouse-like quality. The vibe was good, so I stayed.

"I swear I don't ever do stuff like this. I've never done anything like this in my entire life, actually," I said.

"What's your name?" she asked.

Nick May

The first week, we flirted a lot. She was into me, dude. We walked to lunch every day. The second week, the bookstore disappeared. We made out a lot. The third week, she was my girlfriend and I had the best music, the best weather, the best clothes and the best thoughts. I didn't love her. I just liked her a lot. There were things that happened that almost caused me to commit. The first time she wove her arm through mine in public without just trying to get my attention, I knew she had made a connection, and I liked that. I knew it would end just like every other thing I'd ever been in. They all start just like this, but you're feelings say, "Oh, hell, man. Forget about it. That's later!" Later there were always fights, then distance, then the split. I'm sure Dee was the same. She would have done me in eventually.

We never got to the bad parts. We got right to a really good part and then she got in that wreck. That hurt for a while. She was probably doing something completely normal, too. Everyone texts and puts on makeup and looks for CDs while they're driving. You do it because no one else can do it as skillfully as you can. I never found out if she actually was texting or driving with her knees or reading a book or doing something of the sort that might've cause her to crash. I wouldn't have known who to ask. She was only a part of me for like three weeks. I guess I could compare it to the feeling of dropping a new iPhone in the bay. Up to that point, I'd never owned an iPhone, but I was sure it would've been a fierce and swift loss; letting go of something so fast that you probably could have grown a strong attachment to. I know that's materialistic, but it's the best I've got—that and dropping a plate of food.

Dee was dead and I'd never get to the part where she ends things with me for another guy. We'd never get to the part with the "mutual" break up. We'd never get to the part where we fool around or have sex and end up complicating things to the point of perpetual frustration. We'd never get to the part where I see her for the first time with another dude, or the part where she becomes way too invested in her new romantic progress to be concerned with how I'm doing, or the part where she gives me some lame reason for wanting me back, or the part where we almost call the whole thing off over disagreements about wedding music, the part where she forgets my birthday, or I forget our anniversary, or where we realize she can't have kids. We'd never get to the part where she gets pissed at me for buying dumb shit. We'd never get to the part where we start to look different to each other, or the part where we die together. We'd never get to all that stuff.

I guess most of the time when somebody loses someone, they end up going through some sort of mourning period, whether they realize it or not. If it's someone like a close family member or even a girl that you dated for longer than a month, you probably immediately start crying. You ask yourself all kinds of questions. You probably start to hate God if you didn't hate him already. You lose the taste for food, work, school and everything else. None of that happened to me. Losing Dee was like losing at poker. You know going into it that you'll more than likely be returning home with nothing close to what you brought. Dee was a gamble that I knew I'd probably lose—an extra ten bucks I had lying around. Don't get me wrong—ten bucks can be turned into something really good; in fact,

I had probably started winning the poker game before I finally lost it.

Anyway, after Dee was gone, I found a new place to sludge around. The pleather was remarkably cleaner, the dudes wore suits, and the girls shined the steel with no hands. Well, they had to use their hands to start off, I suppose. I later learned that the place was called No-Hands Fran's because the citizens of Indian River often needed to be reminded to keep their parts to themselves. If you need me to spell it out for you, No-Hands was a strip club. Well, it wasn't so much a club as it was a building with naked girls inside. There wasn't a membership or anything; in fact, if half the kids in town had known how lax the place was about carding people for anything, it would have quickly become the choice over the Dairy Queen on Semin (the road was actually called Seminole, but some drop-out thought it would be funny to spray paint over part of the sign.

I only started going in there because there was a dancer who looked a lot like Dee. I mean, if I looked close enough, you know, through the laser beams and smoke, I could tell the difference. This chick was about ten years older and had a birthmark near her left eye. She was attractive—about as attractive as a stripper could be—but she definitely had that stripper stress on her. You know how you can be dropping your kids off at school or pushing a buggy down the aisle at Walmart and you just know that the woman kissing her ninja turtle goodbye or bending down for the cheap bag cereal is a stripper because of how tired and used up she looks? That was B Nocturne. B wasn't her real name, of course, but she never told anyone what it stood for. We all assumed Nocturne wasn't legit either because of how clever it was—she swears that part is real. If it was real, it was the only real thing about her (on the outside at least).

"If you can guess how many times I've gone under the knife, I'll give you a free one, buddy." That was the first thing she ever said to me.

"Fourteen?" I guessed. Her jaw dropped. The howls and laughter stopped for a brief moment as the trance music kept pumping beneath B's soft voice. I caught a glimpse of a Playboy bunny tongue ring.

"Alright, buddy. I owe you one. Let me know when." The guys roared.

My first sort of date with Dee was during one of her lunch breaks at Box-Ear. After visiting, texting and talking for three or four days straight, I hung enough brain to ask her to lunch. She said she never had too long of a break, so I volunteered to pick something up that we could eat in my car. Looking back on that, it seems incredibly odd of me. Maybe it's worse that she agreed to have a near stranger bring her lunch to eat with him in his truck. Anyway, here we were. Dee was sitting next to me, eating like she'd known me forever.

"I don't even like you that much," she joked.

"Well, that's not weird. The girl I brought lunch to yesterday said the same thing."

"Oh, really? Sounds smart," she joked.

"Yeah, I'm actually meeting her soon, so if you could hurry up, that'd be cool," I said.

"Douche," she replied.

She was late as hell getting back to work that day. We got into some conversation about how soon was too soon to say you're dating. Man, the best thing about Dee was that she never played hard to get. The girl knew we clicked from the second we met and she never played games. She wasn't ashamed of being vulnerable. She put her self out there and held nothing back. The least I could do was give her the same.

"Can we please do this tomorrow?" she asked smiling.

"Of course," I said.

Okay, here's the thing—anywhere else, I would have looked right past B as a girl my brother's age who had seen her prime and let it go a while back—but in here, B was a diamond. There wasn't a dude in the room who would have let her walk away like I did without immediately taking her up on her offer; in fact, most of the guys who had begged for some private time with B ended up getting one of her younger understudies. B had a school of young women under her tutelage who she not only taught how to take clothes off but also helped to put those clothes on in the first place. Miss Nocturne was more of an inner-city missionary than any priest from St. Luke's ever hoped to be.

This is what B did: imagine a girl gets kicked out of her home by her parents for doing something innocently wrong like drinking underage, smoking a joint, or sneaking out (this is a best case scenario, by the way). The girl takes a job at a less-quality place than Fran's (yes, there were less-quality places) strictly because of the sheer amount of money she could get from dancing. A patron of the establishment picks her up. Patron becomes boyfriend. Boyfriend becomes pimp. Before you know it, this chick is being peddled all over town like a rag doll and beaten to hell on her off-days. B had young guys, strong guys (a position that I was completely eligible for) who would rescue these

10

said girls from said situations. It would only be a matter of time before she would offer me a position.

B had this idea that so long as the girls were being treated fairly, not overworked, not underpaid, and got to sleep in a warm bed, that being a motherly pimp wasn't such a bad thing, especially if she could turn a profit from it. B was never one of those cult stories you see on 90s sitcoms where the Moses figure tricks his disciples into trusting him and then ends up having done it all for money. The girls knew that B was making money off of them, but they were handsomely paid, so it didn't matter. B was the real deal. The most important thing to her was making sure that if these girls felt like they had to do what they were doing in order to take care of themselves or their kids, that they sure as hell had better be doing it in a manner that was, at the very least, a little more safe and civil. B gave them clothes, food, beds and transportation. B's dudes were more than just rescue rangers. They were tailors, short-order cooks, butlers and ferry boys. The dynamic was good between the guys and the girls. Everyone was getting paid, but having the males cater to the females was all a part of B's plan to make the girls feel like they were worth something. The guys didn't mind. Whether it was because of previous man-damage or the presence of true compassion, the guys received affection from those girls in just about every way imaginable.

"I think I'm in like with you," I told Dee one afternoon. What the hell did that mean?

"I think I'm in like with you, too, Thom," Dee laughed. Ok, I guess that did make sense. Right then, lying on her Strawberry Shortcake sheets, it was like I captured all those butterflies in a gas chamber and watched them drop to their deaths. I kissed her damn good. And she kissed me back. I hadn't twisted her arm into anything. I hadn't won her over. She was sold, like I was, from way back on the Test Prep aisle. My life had previously been consumed by the idea that you chase girls. The chase is hardly ever neutral and girls never ever chase you. The man is the hunter. If the girl can stand you, she may let you bag her for a while, but you better be able to constantly reinvent yourself in order to keep her. That was my understanding. I was in disbelief with how well things were going. Dee had to be a ghost. A dream. A figment. Something had to be wrong with this. Something wrong with me. Something wrong with her.

"That's your catch isn't it?" she whispered, as we sat watching previews in the theatre.

"What?"

"You don't like popcorn. That's your catch."

"Yeah, that's it. I'll see you later," I said as I faked standing to leave. She pulled me back down by the arm, laughing. She held my hand the old way—like brothers do during prayer.

All in all, B had nine or ten guys working for her. Most remained nameless during that time, but a few of them stuck out to me as B's main "Pieces" (as I liked to call them). First, there was Soo. Soo was a 60-year-old Korean who handled most of B's higher affairs. If there was business that only traversed lips through whispers, Soo was most likely the guy who handled that. Next, there was Samson, the bartender. B called him Sam for short. Aside from a long list of house duties,

Sam was the guy who micromanaged the club when B was gone. Sam's body was like a hairless meat truck full of whale blubber. He was always in an apron covered in what I swore had to be bloodstains. Sam ran the kitchen and the dormitories for the girls who actually kept residence at the club. Lastly, there was Combs, a wiry, middle-aged fellow with dark hair and glasses. Now, Combs was a special case because other than overseeing B's finances, I can't really put a finger on what exactly it was that he did, but I knew it was important. Everyday he brought B a fresh, oversized postal envelope, and left with what looked like a giant-ass hardback brail Bible. It was the kind of book you just assume has a gun-shaped or money-sized hole cut into it. B had it set like this so she didn't have to pay too much attention.

B paid special attention to me—real special attention. Beyond just going out of her way to find excuses to pull me back to the "special" room, I could tell she was planning something big for me. I guess she saw that I wasn't really in there for the explicit nature of the place. She saw me as someone she could trust with her little dolls. The first favor I did for B was when she threw me the keys to the Rubicon and asked me to take Bobbie down Semin. I didn't think twice about it being my initiation or my signature on B's contract of faith and fealty. Bobbie was our token blonde flagship. You've seen her. I'm sure you don't need a description. She didn't talk to me a lot. Not just yet. The place where I dropped her off ended up being just a house in a nice suburb.

"This your place, Bobbie?"

"Oh, no, just a friend's place. Thanks, Tombo!" That was a nice one. Bobbie coined it, herself. As she exited the G.I. Green Jeep, I noticed several other girls that I recognized from No Hands standing around the exterior of the house—smoking cigarettes and texting. I didn't want to know what was going on inside. Several months later, Memory would swear that a friend had shown her a dirty internet video that featured me in a Rubicon. I never watched it. Too much for me to stomach. It could have been any of the hundred times I dropped girls off at the house that month, but I never got out of the car.

Dee never let me take her home. Sometimes, she'd vaguely answer a question about where she lived and quickly cover it up by mentioning all the different places she'd moved to and from.

"So, do you still even live with your family? This is something about you that I have no clue about!" I was just puzzled.

"I've told you this, Thom," she insisted.

"No, you haven't. Are your parents together or divorced?"

"Divorced and remarried. Twice each. My half-sister and I lived together for a while, but then she moved in with her boyfriend." Dee was eating a bagel in the back of Box-Ear. I was sitting beside her, half watching a pedo-card game down the way.

"So. Who. Do. You. Live. With?" I obnoxiously asked again.

"My. Dad," she replied.

"Is he cool, or?"

"Yeah, he's cool. He let's me be who I be."

I laughed. For some reason, I didn't believe it. I think it was my instinct kicking in. I'm a rescuer, man.

Not only could I see myself in an honest-to-God relationship with Dee, but I also wanted to rescue her from whatever the hell kind of situation I assumed she was in. I watched her carefully finish her bagel, wiping the corners of her mouth, never looking up. She sat close to me. I had never envisioned Dee being the kind of girl that needed to feel safe. Sure, you say, "all women want to feel safe." No they don't. A majority of women want to either be with someone who makes them feel dangerous (a bad boy) or independent (another woman). If women wanted to feel safe, there'd be a whole lot less of us nice guys crying in our rooms listening to Chris Carrabba.

Before long, B had me trucking girls all over town. Most of the destinations were normal. Hair places. Nail places. Plastic Surgeons. The house on Semin. Occasionally we'd visit a sort of creeper joint but nothing too serious. The girls literally got in the car and told me where to go. Up until then, I hadn't seen any money for my troubles. I honestly didn't mind that much. I never had to pay for gas, and trucking hot girls around all day was enough to keep me interested. Then Deion hijacked me. Deion was a muscle-bound black dude who led B's little commando group that would go on top secret missions and come back to No Hands with new girls from time to time.

"Thom. Need the Jeep," Deion commanded late one night as he marched toward the vehicle with a handful of dudes who looked like clones. I put my fourth-meal on hold as they piled in and closed the doors.

"Marina," he barked. Apparently, Deion had gotten a tip about a guy who lived in a small house down by the slips and was keeping two girls chained up like a couple dogs. There was supposed to be a gray car in the driveway to mark the house; instead, there was a brown El Camino, but Deion was sure it was the place. He gave some quick instructions before he and the rest of the guys unloaded silently from the Jeep and disappeared around the back. Several minutes later, the front door swung open, and a Super Mario-looking character came pouring out of the house wearing nothing but Fruit of the Loom and running shoes. He was yelling, "I'm not him! I'm not him!" He got to the first step before Deion got ahold of the back of his neck and brought him down.

I watched for several seconds as Deion sat on the guy in that yard and laid into him one fist after another. I listened. All was quiet in the cool night except for the dull sound of Mario's face breaking apart and his occasional semi-conscious vocal reactions to each blow. It got awkward quick. Deion must have seen something in there that spurred it on. Then, as the rest of the guys rounded the back of the house with the two mangled girls, I got the picture.

I wasn't surprised after that when B started slipping rolls of ones into my pants during our alone time. Let me clarify exactly what our "alone time" consisted of—it was basically me sitting on a non-reclining recliner while she sat on the arm and asked me how I was doing in a very sexually compromising way.

"I'm fine. Yep. Doin' good," I'd say, praying she didn't take anything else off.

"Thom, you're a sweet kid." Why was she calling me a kid? I was probably eight years younger than she was. "I don't know why I always call you kid. You're probably, what, only … five years younger than me?"

"Yeah, probably," I'd say. "How old are you again?"

"Thom, I need you to do me a favor."

"Alright," I replied. "What's up? Need me to run one of the girls to the underwear store?"

"That's funny, Thom. I was actually hoping you could pick something up for me ..." In my newly adopted profession, "pick something up" could be anything from a burger to a future stripper—you never know. B continued.

"There's a guy who lives in Pinehelm who owes me a little bit. I know that sounds bad, but he knows you're coming, and he's completely prepared to give you what I need. All you have to do is run over there and grab it. Really, it's not even like he owes me. He's just donating to me. Very charitable dude."

"Pinehelm," I restated.

"Yeah, yeah. 105 Bellview. You know where that is?"

"Yeah. Yep," I replied, grabbing the keys and backing out the door. Anything to get me out of that room. I was only a man, after all. The place B had me going wasn't far. Sort of a small sub-city on the south end of Indian River proper. The only reason I had any clue where to find Pinehelm was because Dee took me to a park down there once to make out. She said it was somewhere she and her sisters used to come play when they were younger.

No commandos today. I was alone. No big deal, Thom. Just walk up, ring the doorbell and ask a dude for money, or drugs, or bodies or whatever. I circled the house a couple times before I halted on the front curb. The place was shady at best. The lawn hadn't been mowed in years—literally years. The roof on the brown brick 70s era burb pad was still covered from end-to-end with a blue FEMA tarp. Ivan was like six

17

years ago. Probably the last time old Joel cut his grass, anyway. Sorry, yeah—Joel was the name of the guy I was hitting up for B. The mailbox, a shitty old tin can bent halfway to the street read "JUSTICE." This was getting better and better. Less than a month ago, I was on my way to becoming what I always wanted—an artsy, indie significant other with a B.A. in some sort of humanity, and now, I was running "errands" for pimpesses, collecting from dudes with names like Joel Justice. I was about to get my ass beat. I took the keys out of the ignition and stared at the front of the house—wishing I had Deion with me. I was willing to bet a hundred bucks that this guy would be wearing a wife-beater. I decided I'd knock. It was far-less abrasive that way. Then I'd stand back—way back.

I bush-wacked my way to the front door and rapped lightly. A dog barked inside. Sounded small enough. I could hear talking but couldn't make out what kind of people were in there. The locks began to unlatch one deadbolt and chain after another. Sounded like Don Quixote was dry-humping the other side of the door in a full suit of mail. The door opened. Wife-beater. You can mail me a hundred ones to No Hands Fran's via thong.

"What can I do for you?" asked the man I assumed to be Joel. He was wearing this white, plastic jumpsuit like the guys from E.T. unzipped and hanging at his waist. It was some sort of BP temp worker gear from what I could tell. He stood in a pair of large and half unlaced boots. His long hair hung in front of his face like a veil on an ugly bride.

"Hey, how ya doin? I'm Thom. B sent me over?" he looked at me for a second with his mouth half open and then turned to the inside of the house.

"Zack!" a shoeless, shirtless young boy appeared in the hallway behind Joel. He was wearing some brand of Walmart swim trunks by the look of them. Joel looked at him, "Grab me my wallet off my dresser." Wow. This was going to be easier than I thought. I didn't say anything more. I just waited quietly, occasionally pretending to look at my phone like I was getting text messages or whatever. I wasn't a businessman. I wasn't a friend either. I seldom ever actually assumed this position. The only people I ever occasionally got texts from were my two older brothers looking for jobs. Joel had disappeared into the house and left the door gaping open. Just then, my phone actually buzzed. It was B. She was calling to make sure I wasn't dead, I suppose. I flipped the thing open and answered quickly.

"What."

"Thom, get out of there!"

"What? Why?!" I said, backing away quickly and feeling for my keys on my carabineer.

"Joel's on the other line. He's pissed. He thinks you're my new boyfriend." By this time I was running full-speed back through the lawn jungle towards to the Jeep.

"And why would he be pissed about that?!"

"Because Joel is my ex."

"Shit, B!" I hung up and leapt across a ditch toward the passenger side when I heard a bear of a voice from the front door of the Justice residence.

"Hey!" I turned back right as Joel Justice expertly hurled some shiny object at me. A 12-inch throwing knife with a camo hilt pierced my right front tire, crippling my escape. My eyes widened as he reached to his leg holster for another. I slung across the front of

19

the Rubicon and opened the door. I was going to live. The house on Semin seemed like a cakewalk compared to this. I could feel my phone vibrating in my pocket, but the rush of adrenaline was causing me to subconsciously tune it out. I turned the key as a rock smashed the passenger window and hit me on the side of my eye. I went dizzy for a second as I threw the Jeep in reverse and ran straight over that ugly-ass mailbox. Somewhere, whilst wiping the blood from my face, I caught a glimpse of that kid again, standing there looking amazed. Joel was screaming and running towards the car. I kicked it into drive and actually smelled rubber burning as I wheeled down the street going as fast as possible. I could hear the tire flopping and the engine doing overtime, trying to compensate for the car's gimpy leg. The last thing I saw in the mirror was Joel Justice giving me the "suck it" gesture.

Dee and I were sitting in the park on a pair of swings, half necking—half whispering sweet nothings to each other like the gayest jewelry store commercial you've ever seen. Almost three weeks had gone by and I hadn't heard another peep about any of Dee's family. I wasn't complaining. The last girl I had been with was the daughter of the real damn Nightmare on Elm Street. This woman was an overbearing, manipulative, judgmental, two-faced yak-muncher. Dee's life was a true breath of fresh air. After spending forever trying to please parents instead of furthering my relationships, God had given me a girl with no family. I was her family. And she was mine.

We were in that phase where you dig up all the dirt you can on the each other. How many people have you slept with? Have often do you get drunk? How much porn have you watched? All of which were questions that just made me look more and more novice with each answer I supplied.

"Have you ever done like serious drugs?" I asked innocently.

"Yeah, actually, at one point, I got so addicted to heroin that they had to send me to that clinic in Arizona to give me safe doses in order to wean me off of it."

"You're joking. Bet?" Bet was our safety word. If you were lying and the other person called you on it by saying "Bet," you had to tell the truth or you'd never be trusted again.

"No, ok. No, I haven't done anything serious," she admitted.

"Is there really a place like that?" I asked.

"Like what?"

"Where they give you drugs to get you off of drugs," I specified.

"Yeah! Yes!" She replied.

"That sort of makes me sick," I said

"Well, Thom, if they didn't have people administering these 'safe' doses to them everyday, they'd go out and shoot up until their brains exploded. There has to be some sort of way to make their addictions safe." We stared at each other in silence "… Geez, what the hell did I just say? I'm starting to sound like my sister!"

"What?"

"Don't worry about it. I love you, Thom." There it was, as casual as a nod. Firsts. They always catch you unprepared. The way she said it smiling, only focusing on me for the words, I thought I had misunderstood her. She added it like a wink after a joke and just went on swinging like she'd been saying it for years. Like I didn't owe her anything. She said it because I had been scared to. She said it because when you slam your damn fingers in the car door, you don't wait six months to scream bloody murder. You do it right then.

My eye-bone was freaking killing me. That was it. I was done with B's garbage. I wasn't about to become one of her dudes, doing laundry, cutting the crust off of peanut butter and jellies, running chicks all over creation and getting my ass kicked by ex-boyfriends. I pulled into No Hands, locked the Jeep and pushed through the front door. B was waiting. Deion and a few of the guys were standing around the bar. B came rushing towards me with a slight smile, holding her arms out.

"Thom ... I'm sooo sorry!" She put her hand right on my eye.

"Ouch! Dammit!"

"Ah! Get him some ice!" she yelled. Three guys slid over the bar. "What happened?!" B demanded.

"You're psycho boyfriend threw a rock at my face! Right after he slashed the tire with a throwing sword!" I harshly replied, taking the ice from a faceless piece.

"Oh, man. I shouldn't have asked you to do that," B said, no longer smiling.

"B, I think I'm going to have to call it a day ..."

"That's fine, Thom. Do what you need to do. We'll see you in the morning," B said, turning to walk away.

"No, B, I don't think you get what I'm saying. I'm not coming back. I'm done with all this. You can find someone else to deliver your mail and collect your taxes and all this other horse shit," I said as I sat up and headed for the door. B turned and followed me in a panic.

"Thom! Thom! Thom, come back! Come here. Listen." I stopped, as she turned from the bar to me and back to the bar. "Get a couple blankets and put them on the V.I.P. couch!" and back to me "Listen, Thom." She came closer. "Let me talk to you, ok? We need to talk." I lowered the ice from my eye.

"B, I don't need a dance. I need to go home," I said as I reached for the door. B grabbed my arm. "Thom, please." The whole place stood in silence, like time had stopped. Several of the guys shooting pool were leaning on their sticks in the back. Lady Gaga was playing.

"Alright."

Within moments, B had me sitting on the couch in the special room with three blankets over my lap.

"Getting stoned in my eye doesn't make me cold, B." This singular event had given me a great deal of boldness with her. For whatever reason, my anger combined with her apparent desperation made me brave.

"Thom, I'm sorry about what happened, but I need to tell you some things. First of all ..." For the next twenty minutes I just sat there and listened. About half the time, I was focused on what B was saying, and the other half, I was focused on her left boob that kept slipping in and out of this black, silk robe she was wearing. Why the hell was she wearing that? Then I got to thinking; this was probably the most clothed I'd ever seen her. "... and I just don't think I could do what I'm trying to do without a person like that here with me. I could have any of these other guys do it. I could have Soo do it, but he can't even speak English." It was true. Soo's vocabulary was limited to the phrases "Ok, less go," and "I no know." B kept on.

"When you came in here, I could see it was probably the last place you wanted to be which tells me one thing—you've got a solid heart, man. You're not in here cause you're a pervert. You're not in here because you want to supplant me and start another ring in this town. You're here because somewhere back there you hit Rock Bottom and I was elected to put you back together. For God's sake man, you won't even touch Lina. The girl's all over you, and I don't know if you've seen Lina, but hell, I'd do her. That's trust you can't buy." It was true. Lina was a marvel to behold, but she was dumb as a brick.

"So what are you saying B?"

"I'm saying I want you to stick around and be my dude."

"Your dude?" I questioned.

"You know, like my main … assistant … dude," B stumbled.

"What about all these other guys? Surely you've got some sort of hierarchy here!"

"No, Thom. I'm the Queen. What I say goes. I say the word and they're yours."

From where I was sitting, I could see the rest of the guys going back about their business in the main room, getting things ready for tonight. Several of the girls had arrived and were walking through the V.I.P. room towards the back, looking at me all the while and wondering what was happening. I looked from them back at B. I sat silent for a moment.

"… Ah, whatever." B let out a squeal. "But I want to make a couple hires," I said.

"Anything," B said as she hugged me firmly. Her implant was aggravating my eye. At this point, I was just so pissed, I didn't care what I was agreeing to, so long as I got to see Joel Justice again on my terms. Soo came in with the house phone and held it to B's ear.

"Wha? What? Who is it?" She swatted at the phone like it was a pesky fly.

"I no know," Soo said exiting as B took the phone.

"Hello? ... Hi." There was a long silence. "What? ... When? ... No, not really. I hadn't heard from her in like three years." Someone was dead. By the look on B's face it wasn't anyone she cared too much about. "Well thanks for letting me know ... shit." She hung up the phone. "My half-sister died in car wreck last week. Apparently no one bothered to tell me."

"Why don't you seem upset?" I asked.

"Ah, I wasn't really that close to her. I sort of put her out when I moved in with Joel." My heart stopped.

"Yeah. I'm pretty sure I know her," I said calmly.

"What?" B replied.

"What's her name?" I asked.

Book II

JOHN

She was doing a fine job of causing me to wish I was dead. They told me the first year would be the hardest. First year? Hell, there wasn't going to be a second year! I was basically already married to her for five years anyway if you think about it. Kristy was the kind of girl that you just battle with perpetually—the kind of girl that you just marry because deep down, you know you're probably not going to get anything better—the girl that you stay with because everyone expects you to. You even come to expect it from yourself.

To be honest, the reason she had me waiting to have sex with her for so long really wasn't because of some deep-rooted religious conviction of hers. She was pretty much locked away. Her dad was basically a bigger part of her life than I had really anticipated. My dad wasn't ever around in that capacity, so I just assumed that Lane, her dad, wouldn't be either. I don't think it's really that stereotypical to say that girls with bum dads usually turn out to be hobags. I was more of a ho than she was. Before I was sixteen, Kristy had me going to church every Sunday and Bible study every Tuesday with some ill-conceived hope that I'd get to feel her up on Saturday. I'm not super proud of that, but damn, I've got needs.

Her brother loved me because I drove him and his friends anywhere they wanted to go. Her mom and dad loved me because I worked in a suit, had an apartment, drove an SUV and pretended to like college football. Kristy loved me because I made her feel less inadequate against her other debutante friends. I can't say that I really dug her friends that much. They probably meant well, but man they were bitchy. There were times when

I thought seriously about physically harming a few of them. As far as Kristy goes, there were some good occasions somewhere in there before all this happened. There was a side of me that didn't always crave satiation. I actually didn't mind it when we'd watch a movie in her living room—even if her parents were around, passively keeping us six inches apart. I liked holding hands in church, even if it did make me feel super gay. Everything else I liked about Kristy soon became things only having to do with her body.

I guess her parents were the stupid kids in math class, because apparently no one thought an eight-month pregnancy was weird.

"Man, we've talked about this before! You can't get a girl pregnant through your clothes!" Gil screamed, as we barreled down County Road 1.

"I know, you douche—"

"Oh, hell, man. You know Lane is gonna beat your ass …" Gil said, laughing.

"Well, we're still getting married, man, so it doesn't matter." There wasn't really a second after that that wasn't downhill. The events that culminated in Kristy's pregnant situation were like a string of brick walls being pounded through until we finally got to that one night. I was asked to house-sit for a friend at the church, and Kristy was the first thing that popped into my head. She had just gotten into a huge fight with her parents, and I could tell she was hot about doing something that would piss them off and make her feel like she wasn't a little girl. It took all of ten minutes to move from the front door, to sex, to full-on, regretful separation on our youth pastor's bed. I could tell the dynamic of "losing" her "purity" bothered Kristy a lot—a lot more than it bothered me. I was just relieved that we'd be married and covered long before she started to show. I stopped caring that we were apparently the True Love Waits poster children of our church. Half of those kids were rolling around with each other on the weekends anyway, from what I hear. I wasn't even thinking about being a dad yet. Honestly, it sounds terrible, but all I could really think about was getting a ring on Kristy's finger so we could do it again without the guilt.

Kristy always talked about planning her wedding. I think the last thing she really expected was that she'd have to do it in emergency-mode without allowing it to appear like an emergency. I made a lot of excuses to not be around. I worked a hell of a lot of overtime. I played it off like I was just being responsible, but I really just couldn't stand being around Kristy and her mom. She was so naggy right then, blowing her lid about everything—my personal hygiene, my hobbies, my unsuitable aspirations. I couldn't take it. Besides, what kind of guy has any sort of input about flowers, tool and cake? Chocolate. Give me a damn chocolate cake.

I would see Kristy watching those teen mom shows on MTV during that whole time. She felt really sorry for herself. I stopped caring so much. She could think what she wanted. I just let her be mad at me—so long as I wasn't around for the planning of what seemed like the last day of my life. I could do the waiting for more sex. In all honesty, aside from Kristy turning into a bright white nightmare, the premarital sex wasn't really the problem (despite what our church had beaten into our heads). Sometimes I felt like if things had been different, we would've been fine. That is to say, if we had never, as children and young adults, experienced that detrimental series of fear-fostering instructions that caused so many of our friends to never return to

31

church after failing to stall love or disarm lust's clever, love-colored alias.

We had been officially married for a month now and it really didn't feel any different. The sex didn't even sell me. Kristy seemed to hate it anyway. The baby news was out. We were in the clear, so I could rest easy. I did actually have some newly adopted responsibilities, though. I had to castrate my apartment. I'd be in there cleaning on a weekend; moving my drums out, throwing away old food, trying to burn out that fart smell with Yankee candles—and she'd come blowing in, carrying on a conversation with me that she had apparently started with herself back in the car. I'd just listen as she berated me for being so fail at life.

"John, why is there cat food all over the floor?" I kept it pretty cool.

"Kris!" I yelled. "It's really hard to control what your damn animals do! There's only so much to learn about cats from YouTube. Nice to see you!"

"Yeah, that's funny," she said. "Maybe you can learn more about cats from the one you play on World of Witchcraft or whatever." I scratched my head.

"I don't understand … are you seriously upset because your dumbass cat can't keep his food in his bowl?!"

"Well, actually, if you care, it's a girl," she said.

"And when were you going to tell me this!?" I asked.

"… The cat," she added. "The cat is a girl, John."

"I haven't played WoW in a month!" I yelled.

"You were on there last week," she argued.

"No I wasn't. I'll show you," I said. "I ran out of game time."

"I'm going to a movie," she sighed.

"With who?!" I asked.

"Brian and Caddy," she replied. "You wanna go?"

"No," I answered.

"Yeah. That's what I thought."

"Kristy, I do all kinds of stuff with you and your friends. Don't give me crap about one time, because I've got my own things to do."

"Oh, what are you going to do, have a raid?" She knew how to cut me deep and make me feel stupid for real.

"Actually, I was hoping to have practice, but Brian's going with you guys? That's cool."

"Well, at least you did one thing I asked and put your drums in the garage," she said.

Kristy made me cram my hobbies into the garage so she could have room for her minimalist lifestyle. She also had scrap-booking stuff all over the place. There is nothing worse than a girl who scrapbooks. Just go ahead and get that in your heads, ladies. Until women figure out how to produce asexually, and you can marry each other and fully appreciate the mess that is scrapbooking, you might as well file that away with cats. Cats and scrapbooks. Those two things will be found in the inner circles of Hell.

"Kristy, I've been working my ass off around here! I go to work for eight hours at your dad's, then I come straight here and start cleaning my house that I pay for while you're out with your mom looking at paint swatches and sniffing baby powder!"

"Ok, first of all, John, all you do for my dad is sit in a chair and type on the computer. I'm at the store all day, on my feet, from five to five and then I start working on baby stuff!"

Nick May

"You have no idea what I do everyday! No idea!" I flipped the computer chair. Bad Idea. Kristy didn't respond well to my fits of rage. She didn't respond at all, in fact. She took it as her cue to leave. But it wasn't like an "oh, I'm leaving because I'm scared" kind of thing. She made it known that she was leaving because she thought I was acting like a child. That's what made me even crazier. Kristy thought it was always, always wrong to be that angry, no matter what. She acted as if she had some sort of internal shutoff valve that kept her from ever becoming irrational.

"How can you leave right now?!" I demanded. "How can you feel good about your night, leaving this situation the way it is. You haven't even touched me in like a week!"

"I'm late," she said calmly. "I have to go."

"No you don't! Screw them!" I yelled. "Who cares about a damn movie when this is happening right now?! We're in a fight right now, I'm upset, and you're just walking out the door!"

"John, I have to go."

"Fine! Go! I don't even remember what started all this, and you may think it's insignificant, or that I don't deserve to have you talk it out with me, but it's a big deal to me! Whatever! Go!"

Kristy turned and walked out the door, simple as that. Now, that was the moment when she was actually supposed to take her hand off the knob and put her things down and talk it out. That's what relationships do, I think. From what I've gathered, if you care about another person at all, you put aside your agenda for one damn second and you clear it up! I lost it. I opened the door and rounded the corner. She was walking down the stairs to the parking lot.

"Hey, don't come back! I don't understand why you're acting so ridiculous. You've been like this for the past three weeks! Don't come back until you give a shit about us!" I could tell she was totally embarrassed of me. She just kept walking, pretending I was yelling at someone else. That kind of crap just made it worse. Everything she did—every single way she reacted just made me more and more angry. The fact that I was showing out so much was making me angry. Being angry was making me angry. This was normal, right? Every relationship has these exact types of fights. Yeah, definitely.

My night was ruined. I couldn't think about anything else. I couldn't get anything done. You know how Kristy's night went? Perfect! She wasn't thinking about me or us or this situation, because it wasn't important to her. Being married was more important to her than being married to me. I started to believe that the only reason she was even with me was because she was too much of a weak-ass to defy her parents and be with a guy she was really attracted to, which was probably the guy I was always trying to be and she wouldn't let me be out of fear—if that makes any sense. Needless to say, I was filled with a lot of doubt about us.

She came back that night. It was a testament to her defiance. It was just more proof that she didn't give a damn about anything I said. I heard her unlocking the deadbolt, and I pretended to be asleep on the couch like kids do when they don't want to speak to their parents. She shut the door and stood still.

"John." She didn't care. "John!" I opened my eyes. A key hit me in the face. She walked out. Good game.

Let's pretend I had cheated on Kristy and burned her mom and dad at the stake and sold their eyeballs to demon jugglers … that's pretty close to how I was being treated over the next few months. Needless to say, I quit my job at her dad's office. The absolute worst part—the part that hadn't even begun to hit me from a paternal prospective, was that Kristy had miscarried and I was somehow being blamed. I heard everything from abuse, to stress, to the baby willing itself away from being born into a hostile environment. Were people really serious? I called Kristy three hundred and sixty-seven times in two days. Normally I would call that obsessive, but we had just lost a baby!

The next time I saw her was when we finalized our divorce. She was looking bad, but I was looking worse. She acted to me about like you would act with a friend of a friend—cordial, but distant. I think I was still in that apartment, trying to settle that fight. I could ask a million questions or make a million accusations but nothing would ever come of it. This situation—this relationship, was so lost that it was completely useless for me to even try. The biggest contributing factor for me to come to that realization was the fact that a black hole had formed somewhere around Kristy's life. All her attention was being completely funneled into some unknown realm. I could tell because I no longer mattered on a conscious or subconscious level to her. I just knew. More than likely, it was a new guy. I never pinned it on her to move that fast, but before long, I'd know the truth, and she'd be just as embarrassed as I'd be stunned.

Kristy was on hold. I needed money or I was going to lose my apartment, too. I had caught wind of a cleanup effort they were doing at the beaches to get rid of the occasional tar ball that washed up from BP's oil debacle taking place a hundred million miles away.

Several of my friends were getting paid fifteen dollars an hour to walk down the shoreline for ten minute intervals between thirty minute breaks, looking for signs of pollution. There was a class I took in a hotel conference room with a bunch of dudes that looked way dirtier than me, and before long, I was taking those long walks on the beach that Kristy always nagged me about never wanting to go on. The sun was hot, man. Hot. It didn't help that we had to wear these bright white man-size onesies. Everything was bright and white and blazing.

"How long you been doing this now, Barry?" I asked my search partner as we walked lazily along the water's edge. Barry was probably older than my dad. He looked like the guy on the fish sticks box.

"Couple months," he said.

"You ever find anything?" I asked.

"Nah. Fish," he replied.

"Oh, really?!" I asked excitedly. "Dead ones? Do you report them?"

"Nah," he answered. "You just throw 'em back in."

"Oh," I said. You see, being a Hazwoper, as they were called, was like being an on-call doctor or National Guard. You had to be ready to jump at a moment's notice within a given twelve-hour increment. Every night we'd just sit around in some obscure parking lot in town, awaiting orders or for a call to come in reporting a single tar ball showing up on the beach, and then we'd head out by the hundreds in this massive exodus like happy Egyptians.

It was honestly the easiest job I'd ever had. It kept my mind off of Kristy, but it seemed like we were all sort of waiting for this inevitable tidal wave that was going to wash millions upon millions of gallons of black death all over the beach, causing us to suddenly regret what we had signed up for. There was talk amongst the Hazwopers that if and when that day ever came, it would be easy enough to just move further up the coast to towns that still had a few weeks yet before the toxic bleed showed itself on their shores. Essentially, one could plan to stay several weeks ahead of the oil and continue to get paid for a minimal amount of work. It sounded like a plan to me. All that was fine until the oil did come—until The Moss Head Motel happened.

We were all sitting around that parking lot one night when we got the call. There were several hundred of us. Mostly dudes. Someone had fashioned a beanbag toss and set it up on the far side of the lot. There was a pretty impressive line forming to play the game. We were bored as hell. It was about 2 A.M. when the radio over on the picnic table began spitting out demands. There were coordinates, latitudes and longitudes, words like "sheen," "tar," and "balls," and within minutes, the moving circus was packed up and on its way. Trash floated here and there, and the pack of large busses roared away from the empty lot as we bid farewell to our nocturnal home. There was a strange excitement on the busses to see what the call was all about. The urgency of the voices on the other end was enough to convince half the Wopers that we were being carted straight into dadgum Armageddon. It felt like being flown into battle and dropped onto the front lines of war.

After a ten-minute ride, we unloaded onto a remote concrete slab at the base of an old pier and walked for several more minutes across a range of dunes and sea oats until we heard the ocean. It was very dark and we were unable to see the shoreline. Several teams of men carted as many large rolling light trailers out onto the pier as they could fit. Within moments, the rigs were hooked to generators and the lights came on. Gasps escaped the crowd of onlookers. A vast stretch of the beach, as far as the lights could show, was slathered with baseball-sized tar. Barry let out a grunt of satisfaction.

"What's that, Barry?" I laughed. We walked off in the direction of the mess.

We worked all night—taking breaks far less frequently than we had been previously. None of us were really lazy enough to purposely put off work. I mean, we didn't have a problem stopping to rest, but we worked steadily. The tar balls were about the consistency of wet grease trap fat, and considering the amount of sand we had to shovel off with each one, the weight added up quick. By the time our shift was finished, we were ready to keel over and die. The better part of the beach had been restored to its more cleanly state, but none of us could predict if and when another wave would hit, so we were ordered to report to a different location the following night—one closer to the new spill site.

The new meeting place was the parking lot of The Moss Head Motel. The Moss Head Motel was more like the Bates place than you'd care to know. A mere two stories, the thirty-one-room beach retreat was a shady-looking establishment straight out of the 70s, complete with man-eating roaches, mold-covered bathrooms and a dry pool with a straight up tree growing inside. It didn't take long for us to realize that this was no ordinary lodging. The motel staff was composed of five Filipinos, the manager of which was a half-crippled old guy whose name I never caught. Their duties seemed limited. The old man just walked around with a face. His four employees (the housekeeping staff) were all women who either couldn't speak English or could and refused to. They kept to themselves.

The staff didn't seem to mind us very much (besides the occasional grimace) as long as we minded our own business. I assumed that BP was also paying the old man, which must have been great for him, considering he probably hadn't made fifty bucks on the beach all winter in a spring break town (plus the fact that the beach was now officially drowning in oil). Several of the guys who had instigated the beanbag toss made an arrangement with the motel staff to up their gaming license with sports like Blackjack, Dice and Cockfighting. Rooms 101, 102 and 103 were reserved for those activities respectively. The old man—the one with the face—well, his face changed as soon as the beanbag brothers brought him a stack of bills from the first night's take. After that, I don't think I saw him again.

Barry did some spying for me (though I'm sure he didn't know it). I hung out close to the buses, where the cleaner types stayed awaiting the call of duty and chain-smoking their way to a worse fate than the motel's most diehard subscribers. Every night, Barry would visit each of the quickly multiplying hubs of underground activity and report on their happenings. 103 stayed packed. 101 and 102 basically shared members and had a door that passed between the two rooms. The pros who hung out inside from night to night had come up with an impressive way of monitoring and checking their own system: a rotation of dealers or referees with a house pot that went towards rent for the rooms, the remainder of which was given to the winners of each game. The ref rotation was made of players. If you played, you were, at some point, officiating.

I guess it was sometime during that first week that the Winnebago showed up with all the girls in it. Apparently, they were all stripper/hooker/porn star triple threats from a place in Indian River called Fran's, or at least that's what Barry told me. Before long, whoever was in the Winnebago had also made an arrangement with the motel, because Barry claims to have seen the old man stumble out of there with a wad. The girls spilled out of that thing like a group of Wallstreet brokers on lunch, and in ten minutes, the entire top floor had become inhabited by chicks with names like Nicky, Chloe and Layla. There were eight rooms on each section besides the one with the office and the vending machines, so I knew there had to be at least twenty girls all in all. Needless to say, 101, 102 and 103 thinned out a bit.

Barry was probably their first paying customer. One night while standing by the buses, I remember him saying,

"I'll introduce you," like he knew them. Maybe he did. From everything I heard about Fran's, it seemed like a place that Barry might hang out. Every single one of them had waiting lists a mile long from the first night they arrived. They were getting even less sleep than I had been. The formidable economy of dirty business, newly born in a shit hole like The Moss Head Motel had me drugged—and speaking of which—the new arrival of illicit substance dealers wasn't helping me lose interest in the flourishing compound. I couldn't get a wink of sleep. I was awake for the whole thing, from start to finish, so I witnessed the boom of the motel from its humble beginnings all the way to its abrupt ending.

The Moss Head Motel became the only place anyone spent their BP checks. More and more patrons arrived as the weeks went on—people I'd never even seen before. I just assumed they were new crew, but I never saw any of them at the cleanups. It never really seemed like anyone was taking charge or dominating the place. Stuff just happened, I suppose, the same way riots are formed.

I don't know if it was the excitement of the place, the ever-changing hours or a combination of both that first sustained my insomnia. It seemed like every bit of work or mere observation of the activities at the motel just caused me to be more wide-eyed and awake. To be honest, I wasn't so alarmed by the first few days without sleep. I had done it before, whether in college or in moments of unbridled inspiration where it just seemed pointless to stop creating whatever I was creating. It was only after a whole week with no solid sleep that I began to worry. I'd be down there, watching the birds kill each other or observing how the ladies, one-by-one, invited customers into their lairs amidst the treacherous racket of Wopers and random beach trash hollering at the top of their lungs at card games or in drunken rages. All it would have taken was one honest cop to stop by, see what was happening and shut it all down.

I'd say on any given night, there were more police officers there than anyone else buying into the illegal smorgasbord of activity. In my opinion, that's the reason it all grew so rapidly in that first couple weeks. I honestly couldn't tell you what kind of profit the old man or the Winnebago or the beanbag brothers were turning. The drugs sure were a popular new addition. I always figured it was one of those situations where the actual establishment wasn't making the real money; however, people were paying rent at The Moss Head Motel—I just wasn't sure who. That's what had me occupied most of the time as we waited for or ignored the calls of spills night after night and assumed the roles of gamblers, thieves, addicts and brothelists.

One night in particular, I remember seeing this really young dude—looked seriously like he might be the same age as me, handing out money and pointing out orders the way a contractor would. He wasn't just a nobody, though. People were listening to him. The girls sure were wrapped around his finger. I watched him close. He wasn't a pimp. Didn't dress or act like one. If I didn't know any better, I'd assume they were all his older sisters. That was the type of communication they had, except in a more respectable way. He was taking care of them.

I can't speak for a single time when I ever saw him trying to peddle the girls around or anything. He wasn't a door to door hooker salesman like you'd expect most pimps to be. The thing I noticed him doing the most was collecting them from the various top floor rooms. He'd go from room to room dragging these two big dudes who were always with him. He'd knock. The girls would come out. He never took money, but on several occasions I saw him place a hand on a shoulder and point them in the direction of the Winnebago. That's where my detective work stopped. I saw that happen all the time. I never saw him do anything else, and I'd never see what happened to those girls inside that camper.

"Barry, you ever wonder who's putting all this on?!" I yelled. It was late and raining. Barry turned from a crowd of onlookers cheering at their favorite girls in the middle of a stripper auction. He got down low, put his arm around my shoulders tightly and pointed up at the sign as if spelling out a vision.

"The-Moss-Head-Motel!" Barry often made sarcastic remarks towards me in order to put me in what he thought was my place as a wet-eared Woper. His breath smelled like Listerine, the way beer can smell minty sometimes. He smiled, pat me on my back and turned around towards the show. Forty or fifty guys were in a bidding war to see who would sleep with this blonde with big boots (among other things). I looked back towards the Winnebago.

"No, no, I mean … who is being allowed to put this on?!" Barry looked at me amidst the noise of the crowd, then looked back towards the front and raised his hand. The mock-auctioneer screamed something as soon as Barry's hand went up,

"One fifty once! Twice! Sold to that guy back there that looks like the fish sticks box!" Barry smiled and looked at me.

"Have fun," he said, "and lighten up." In five seconds, I had a rabble of boisterous, oily dudes shoving me towards the front. I felt a soft hand grab onto mine and whisk me off towards a stairwell near the camper. It was the blonde. We had escaped the physical reach of the crowd, though they were still shouting "Jah-ohn! Jah-ohn!" in unison as I tried to pull away. I caught a quick glimpse of the not pimp guy watching me from the far end of the lot where the busses were parked. Within moments, the door shut and the blonde was pushing me onto the bed. The muffled crowd roared and whistled beyond the door.

"Woah! Woah!" I protested. She stopped.

44

"What?" She didn't look trashy like most girls you'd see on the Internet. Well, now that I think of it, some people would probably call her trashy, and I'd put money on her being on the Internet, but she wasn't hard to look at. Let's face it, Hugh Hefner doesn't make millions of dollars because he chooses paper over plastic.

"I just—I'm married. I was married. I am married."

"Thanks for being honest." She kissed me fast and didn't let up. She was wearing some kind of candy lip-gloss but it was gone within seconds of me giving in. I could hear the noise dying down outside as the rain poured harder. More than likely, they'd go inside and continue the madness in 110 where the new meth chefs hung out.

"Stop. Stop. Stop," I whispered. The blonde sat back with her legs still situated across my situation. "When did she get naked?" I wondered. She was looking quite "professional." She never seemed to be impatient—just paused. I breathed, or tried to.

"What's up?" She asked. Putting her hair into a ponytail.

"Nothing. You wanna tell me your name or …?"

"That's sweet. It's Bobbie. John right?" I looked at her, puzzled.

"Oh, right. The crowd. Sorry, I'm just not used to this. I'm all out of breath and you're … well, you're looking very well."

"John, sweetie, just try to relax. Everything's paid for, and I'm a professional." She dove back in. My mind flashed to that night with Kristy that first time. It felt like this—like I was experiencing all the elements or steps of a sexual encounter in one brief instance instead of over a period of several months in middle school

45

like most kids do. This was the kind of stuff that, as a pubescent, young teen, you go to bed hoping you'll dream about. This time Bobbie stopped.

"What do you want me to do?" Now, that was a question that was very open-ended. It's not every day the world smiles upon you like this. That would have been my life every day if Kristy ever felt like doing anything other than drinking coffee and wearing sweatpants that said "Pink" on the butt instead of eating some chocolate and wearing something that wasn't deemed "sexy" by a lesbian softball team.

"Uh, so you've gotta be like twenty-four, twenty-five?" I asked.

"I'm nineteen." She smiled.

"You're, you're nineteen …" I restated. She stared at me. "Were you made by Mattel or have you had work done?"

"The latter." She sat up and crossed her arms, appearing to be the slightest bit offended.

"How'd you ever afford that?" I said, trying desperately to keep conversation going.

"First of all, what are you? Twenty-three?" She asked. "You're wearing a watch that probably cost more than my last semester of classes. How did you pay for that?"

"I see your point," I said.

"They were a graduation present," she added, placing her hands on her waist and looking down at herself from side to side.

"Oh, I see," I replied.

"Not really," she admitted.

"Oh, you didn't graduate?" I asked.

"John, I'm a person who sells her body for a living."

She wove her fingers through mine and lifted my arms above my head.

"Ok," I said, "No more questions. I'm sorry."

"Listen, it's no problem. I have this conversation thirty times a week with guys who can't understand how a hot blonde with a brain isn't dating some rich dude and throwing Gray's Anatomy parties every week for her girlfriends at a condo in Wynn Grove. It's normal. The answer is, I don't work for your typical Chris Brown. I'm a white collar escort who, in all honesty, is a little over-qualified to work in Vegas. That price your friend paid for us to hang out was as good as charity—not to toot my own horn—but that's what Thom needs and you don't ask too many questions when you're a part of a movement whose reach well-exceeds what Oprah does." Bobbie took a deep breath and smiled. I was in love.

"Who's Thom?" I asked. "I'm sorry, did you say have sex with thirty guys a week?"

"No," she replied. "I said I have this 'conversation' with thirty guys a week. I have sex with about fif—"

Suddenly, there was a knock on the door. I looked and saw it wasn't locked, and just then, the not pimp fellow walked in with his two friends. We froze. Well, I froze. Bobbie seemed as cool as she had been the entire time.

"What's up?" She asked, still perched on me like a jockey.

"We need him out," the not-pimp pimp said. Now that I could see them up close, I noticed that he had a wound on the side of his head that looked like it was healing from a pretty serious encounter. I could tell that the two "bodyguards" weren't your typical ruffians elected solely because of their size. These guys weren't lackeys by any means. On most TV shows, figures like these usually played more boring parts—looking like statues, donning matching blazers or assuming that traditional caricature of wearing sunglasses at night. These dudes actually looked borderline normal. All three of them seemed like the kind of young hipsters you were more likely to see in the big city at a My Morning Jacket show. The middle one, who I assumed to be Thom, well he looked disturbingly like me (which was sort of pale and short like a brown-eyed Elijah Wood). Bobbie was getting up to turn on the bathroom light.

"Alright, Johnny-John, can you wait outside for me for a sec?"

"Sure," I said, looking at the guys. "No problem."

"No. You know what? He can come, too," Thom said, looking at me. "Is that cool? Can you come with us really quick?"

"Sure, I mean … what's up? Did I do something, or?"

"No. No. You didn't do anything. That's kind of the point actually," he said. I was confused.

"Oh, I mean, I didn't mean to insult her," I looked at Bobbie standing there, unabashed of anything, "she's great, we just haven't had time to—"

"No, that's not it. I promise. Don't worry. Just come with us real quick. You ready Bob, or you just going naked?"

"I'll just come like this," she said, jokingly, reaching for a towel. The guys smiled.

"Yeah. Right." Thom said, throwing Bobbie what clothes he could scoop up with one hand. This was such a weird experience. It could've also been that fact that I hadn't slept in ages.

Thom and his buds walked us down the stairs towards the mysterious Winnebago. The rain had stopped for the most part, and the busses were gone—along with the crowds of whooping hazwopers—off to the clockwork oil spill that would hit consecutive stretches of the beach every evening soon after midnight. It almost felt like how dumb kids will prank their neighbors but only after midnight because they think 12 A.M. is some sort of sleeping spell which makes them impervious to capture.

There were girls all over the parking lot now, finally released from their offices, having cigarettes and texting their boyfriends or girlfriends or God knows who else. They didn't seem that tired. Who knew how many guys they had been through tonight. The only thing I really cared about now was what was inside that camper. I had wondered for weeks who was behind this portion of The Moss Head Motel extravaganza, and I was finally going to see. I guess it had crossed my mind that it would be a woman. It was a cool twist that I wasn't necessarily expecting when I stepped up into the '80s era motor home.

That was the first time I saw B. She looked around thirty with a tongue ring and a birthmark near her left eye. She was sitting on a small couch reading an issue of *Entrepreneur*. I just remember that image, as if to suggest that what she was doing was an entrepreneurial endeavor. She was junky looking—probably hot at one point, but not anymore. Not to me, anyway.

"Hi, kids. What's up?" she said, putting the magazine down. She was wearing a black, silk shorty robe and pink, fuzzy house slippers. The door shut behind us as we all crunched in.

"Hey. Some older dude bought this guy a date with Bobbie and they didn't get anywhere." B looked at me and reached for some popcorn in a bag sitting next to her on the couch. She'd been chomping on it since we walked in. That's how I noticed the tongue ring that may or may not have had a Playboy bunny on it.

"Well are you gay or is Bobbie celebrating No-Shave November early?" she asked. "You know that holiday's only for guys, right Bob?" Bobbie turned and walked down the short hallway, taking her ponytail out and ignoring the comment. B looked at me, "I'm just messing with her. She knows I'm joking. I love Bobbie."

Shawn and Stacey (which I later learned were the names of the two assistants, both of which were Thom's older brothers) left the trailer as B gave them the signal and then reached for more popcorn. Thom picked up the magazine and sat down on the other end of the couch, looking disgusted as he thumbed through the pages. He spoke through a yawn.

"Yeah, so, anyway, you were saying you maybe needed another piece for Bobbie and I saw this brother, scared to death of her. Thought you might want to meet him," Thom said, flipping intently through the pages of the magazine. B chomped, extending the bag of popcorn towards Thom.

"You want some?"

"Hell no," he replied. B smiled at me, as if she knew that's what he'd say. She swallowed and straightened her face as she looked back at Thom.

"You're suggesting I might want to employ a guy to look after Bobbie who is, in fact, afraid of … Bobbie?" Thom slapped the magazine shut and threw it on the couch.

"Look, if you don't want him, I'll just get them back to business and no big. But you're the one always saying how you want honest dudes in here with good hearts, and he's the first guy I've ever seen hold Bobbie off for that long. He must be retarded or something," Thom said, standing up and walking to a small pot of coffee in the kitchenette. Bobbie came back out and kissed Thom on the cheek.

"Thanks, Thom," she said as she took his former seat on the couch.

"Hey, don't sit—ah …" Thom let out a sigh.

Bobbie had now produced a laptop with an apple on it. She began typing. "So what is it, B? You won't let Johnny-John be my bodyguard?"

"You want him to be your bodyguard?" B asked, looking over at Bobbie. Bobbie looked up at me, straight into my eyes.

"Nah," she shrugged.

"Hey!" I complained. The three of us laughed. Thom was busy with the coffee pot.

"B, did someone just wash these cups?" he asked.

"Honey, I don't think anyone has ever washed those cups. Why?"

"Tastes like cleaner," he said, sniffing the pot. "The coffee tastes like Windex or something."

"Who made coffee?" B asked him.

"I don't know. Pot's on. It's warm. Tastes gross, though, like somebody straight up sprayed Windex in it." B looked back at me, impatiently side glancing back at Thom and smiling.

"Anywaaaaay …"

"Yeah, Thom. QQ about it," Bobbie laughed.

"What does that even mean?" Thom asked, half offended.

Nick May

"It means cry about it," I said, smirking. The room went silent. Bobbie gave me a high five. B and Thom looked at each other. I noticed I was still standing.

"Is it cool if I uh—?" I asked as I pulled the chair from the mini table behind me.

"Oh, sure, sure. Sorry, hun. Have a seat," B insisted. Thom leaned up against the counter and pulled out a shiny, black iPhone. He and Bobbie went about texting and typing as B crunched on more popcorn. The sounds were irritating.

"So, tell me about yourself, John. John, right?" she asked.

"Yeah, John," I replied. "Uh … what exactly do you want to know?"

"Ever worked in girls before?" she crunched.

"Hah, no," I laughed "so am I right to assume that you guys are the hosts here?"

"Well, sort of," Thom answered hastily. "Like, all the girls are ours, and we have an arrangement with the Filipinos, but all the other sort of shady things like the drugs and the gambling—I think those are all just honest by-products of dirty people and dirty business—not to say that we run a dirty business." This wasn't accurate. Remember, I'd done my share of Insomnia-driven research.

"Actually, they were here first, so you guys are the by-products, I think."

"Well, say what you will," B replied, "but, most of our girls could be in way shittier situations right now." I looked at Bobbie as she shut her laptop.

"Done. So, are we gonna do it, Johnny-John, or what? I feel kind of weird. I actually feel like I kind of know you a little bit now, and I'm honestly a little embarrassed to sleep with you."

"Man, you're just real open, aren't you?" I said.

"I'm tired," Bobbie got up, "is it cool if I lay down back there in your bed until you go to sleep, B?"

"Sure, sweetie, just throw that laundry on the floor or whatever."

"Ok. Goodnight," Bobbie said, slapping Thom on the ass as she left the room.

"Goodnight!" Thom and B said in unison. They were both looking at me again.

"Alright, I don't really understand why I'm here," I stated. "Can someone explain—"

"Buddy," Thom interjected, taking a sip. "I've been wondering the same thing since I got here, and I'm sorry, but you don't really get the luxury of answers right now."

"Listen," B spoke. "Here's the deal. Bobbie's a constant case for harassment. Thom's duties are extending a little further from what he was originally hired to do, which was to basically get the girls from point A to point B and watch out for them at the same time," B took a breath "sooo, I'm assuming you don't want to pick up tar for the rest of your life, and since Thomas here seems to have developed some sort of faith in you from the five minutes he's known you, I guess what we're trying to ask is if you'd like a job." B looked into the bag, gathering the last few pieces of popcorn. Thom took another sip of the coffee.

"I'm sorry, that just tastes too much like Windex," he stated, pouring it into the sink.

"Um ... sure. I'll do it," I said, feeling relieved that I'd never have to wear the white jumpsuit again.

"Ok. Cool. Well, I can't give you quite as much as BP is giving you, but the work's easier, so we'll just do what we can," B said. Thom tisked. I looked at Thom as he squeezed into the small bathroom and closed the door.

"That's fine," I said.

"Sweet," B replied. Suddenly, the sound of Thom's pee filling up the plastic toilet bowl became exceedingly loud. B just stared at me with a content smile. I looked around politely, pretending not to notice. Thom's pee reverberated through the small corridor like thunder. It didn't quit. Bobbie emerged from the back, stopping in front of the bathroom. Frustrated, she looked at us.

"Is he serious?!"

Bobbie was a remote worker, so my first night on the job, I had to walk her to her appointments at the motel and stand outside the rooms, making sure nothing happened. I wasn't really sure what I would do if something ever did happen, but I'd be there, nonetheless. It was kind of like being a hall monitor or something—like I'd have anything to say or do about it if some burley Woper ever came along giving me trouble. I just stood there and tried to look as badass as I possibly could.

Is it weird that I was growing a little bit of jealousy for Bobbie? I'll admit it. I sort of had a little crush on her—the way, at some point or another, you develop a crush on your best friend's little sister or something. Maybe Bobbie was as flirty with all her customers as she so often was with me, but I doubt it. After all, I was probably the only dude she'd ever had a $150 conversation with.

I had a plan. I was going to woo Bobbie to me with some sweet charm—treat her like a lady, you know. I wanted to know her story. I was standing there, thinking about all these things and watching some drunk idiots put on show, trying to leap from the edge of the dry pool to the tree growing in the middle, when Bobbie's most recent customer came strolling out of her room. His shirt was unbuttoned. He nodded at me with a straight face. I nodded back. Prick. Bobbie came to the door, naked as usual.

"Aaaand, time!" she joked. I smiled.

"Smells like karate in there," I said, still facing out.

"Yeah, well, it's my dojo," Bobbie replied, pulling up her dress, "what's going on out here?" she asked.

"They're trying to jump on the tree in the pool."

"Idiots," she said, stepping out next to me. She grabbed onto my arm and fixed her shoe. Right about then, I saw a familiar figure show up behind Bobbie. It was Barry.

"Hey, hey, Bare!" I said, "what's up, brother?"

"What's up is I'm about to get my $150 back, or this bitch is gonna take me around the block." I thought he was joking at first, but then I realized he was actually pissed. Barry was always the go-to guy for reason and calm. He was often the great statue that weathers the storm. Bobbie looked at him, playfully frightened and then back at me for some sort of sign.

"Barry, It's cool, dude. I thought that was a gift." Bobbie stepped into the doorway.

"Yeah, well," Barry started, "I was a little drunk then, or maybe I'm a little drunk now—but either way, I'm about to get some kind of return."

"Dude, why are you acting like this?" I asked, shocked. "Look, we'll get you your money back if that's what you want, but don't get all worked up—"

"No. You know what? It's cool," Bobbie spoke up. "Come on in, Barry," she said, stepping aside.

"What? No!" I replied as Barry shoved me up against the rail and walked in.

"John, it's fine. I'll just get this over with and no problem," she assured me, closing the door. I turned to put my hands on the rail, shaking the chain links violently and growling with frustration. Just then, I saw Thom making a B-line across the parking lot. He was alone. I waved my arms, trying desperately to flag him down, but he had already seen what happened and was making his way over with intrepid speed. He swung around the stair rail and leapt up in three or four steps, never stopping to look at me. With one swift motion, he kicked the door in. I don't even know if it was ever locked, but he wasn't checking.

I stayed out but saw Thom reach into the back of his pants, pull out a very real-looking gun and pistol whip Barry right across his fish stick face. Barry rolled off the bed, unconscious. He had made it further with Bobbie than I had. I guess there's not a whole lot of distraction when you're a natural conversationalist like Barry. He certainly wasn't talking now. I never saw a drunk, naked sea lion passed out on a motel room floor before. Bobbie was in shock, again, halfway undressed. I don't understand why she just didn't leave her clothes off.

"Come on," Thom said, extending his hand to her. It was dark inside the room. Thom pulled Bobbie out and aimed her towards the stairs where she vanished down and into the trailer. Thom looked at me, half disappointed, half amused.

"Here," he handed me the shiny silver gun, "don't let dickheads like that mess with her."

"Sorry, dude," I said. "He was my friend. I thought I could reason with him."

"Yeah, well, when he wakes up, maybe you can give reason another try," he replied, walking off down the stairs. Thom was a badass. I looked back into the room at Barry's unconscious figure lying on the floor and then looked down at the gun.

I was a little embarrassed, so I spent the rest of the night wandering. By the time the busses had pulled out and the place quieted down, it was 2 A.M. I once again found myself in a steady state of perpetual awake. The pre-dawn hours are a lonely time. I would lie awake in one of the rooms, the light from a streetlamp outside, shining on my face. I'd think about Kristy for hours and hours. Life seems so much longer when you're not sleeping. When I was younger I would have never imagined that I'd one day go through a time in my life where I'd spend weeks waiting for sleep. A year ago I would've assumed I'd be asleep next to Kristy tonight. Instead I was sitting on the steps in Hell, waiting for Mary Magdalene to come out of her Winnebago. That night in particular was excruciatingly long. I had forgotten sleep.

In the days that followed, I found myself hanging out at the motel long before the sun went down. I got to drive this Jeep that was pretty sick (despite the donut spare and a shattered window). I'd take girls to a house on some road called Semen. Man, that'll never get old. My fiendish crush on Bobbie was still raging. She knew it, too. She would always do little things to feed the flame—things that Kristy would have never done in a million years—things she just would have deemed "slutty." Is it considered slutty if a girl asks you to hand her her bra or untie her dress? I was still trying to woo Bobbie with whatever charm I assumed I had. I was driving her to the community college one day to pay for a class, when I just thought I'd ask,

"So, have you ever had time to date anybody?"

"John, what kind of girlfriend do you think I'd make, sleeping around like I do?" she asked, applying mascara in the visor mirror.

"That's what I'm saying," I added. "You ever stop all this long enough to try?"

"I'll be honest," she began. "No one's ever given me enough incentive to give this up. You're starting to, though."

"What?!" I said, completely bewildered. We had parked at the school. Bobbie put her sunglasses on, slapped the visor back up, took my hand and looked at me.

"You're starting to make me want to quit all this and be your girlfriend," she smiled. Then she released my hand, got out of the car and shut the door.

My phone buzzed. B had programmed the number as someone called Soo. He had been calling me non-stop. Whenever I'd answer, he'd just say, "Dubba-you nye! Come to Fran!" B said that whatever Soo needed was probably important, so I drove over to Fran's while I figured Bobbie would be stalled in drop/add lines. The white gravel crunched as I drove into the parking lot. There were several cars parked around and the front door was wide open. This was home base. It was weird being there. It wasn't really how I pictured my first time in a strip club. I walked in and was immediately greeted by a small Asian man.

"Ok. Less go!" he said, motioning for me to follow. Fran's was a small place with black carpet, black walls and black ceilings. There were ten or fifteen mirror-top tables like you always see cocaine being snorted off of. There was a bar and a single stage with a single poll, but it was a substantial one. As we walked, I observed that there were a few guys scattered around the building doing various house-keeping things. One was mopping the stage. Another was folding clothes, and one guy in a far back room was putting sheets on a bed. Weird. The little Asian man, who I assumed to be Soo, led me to the bar where he produced a W-9 and a pen.

"Dubba-you nye," he said. I got it. There was a huge tank of a man drying glasses behind the bar who looked like he'd just eaten a banana split straight off his shirt. I'll be honest, it had never occurred to me that my job at The Moss Head Motel might be one that required tax information, but I suppose I was really being employed by Fran's, your friendly Indian River strip club.

Soo handed me the pen and walked off towards the back. I stood there and began filling out the cryptic form. W-9s always confused me so much. I looked up at the fat bar guy.

"Do you write 1 or 0 if you want more money back at the end of the year?"

"You claim 0," he said, hanging a wine glass on the rack overhead.

"Right! Thank you!" I replied as I signed the thing and looked around for Soo. About that time, a scrawny-looking hangman with glasses came strolling through the front door and approached the bar carrying a big envelope and a Webster's or something.

"Is she here?" he addressed the barman.

"She's over on Seminole. Where you been?" the barman asked.

"Mission trip," he replied. I had to get used to the weirdness associated with this job. The scrawny guy looked at me, glancing at the form.

"Are you new?"

"Yes," I replied, holding up the W-9.

"You have to bring that back here after she signs it anyway. I'll ride with you."

The ride over to Semin with Combs, as he was called, was awkward to say the least. There are usually two types of people in the world—those who don't mind silence, and those who can't go thirty seconds without making some kind of nonsensical small talk. Combs and I were both the first type. I drove. He sat. The only sound that could be heard was the wind from the broken window. I glanced at him in the rearview as much as I could. His eyes would catch mine every single time. It pissed me off. His left hand fiddled with his phone. His right hand held a giant book and a large pee-colored envelope left open on one end. I won't lie, there were several times I thought about asking what was inside. Combs just didn't seem like the kind of person that would let me peek.

When we arrived at the Semen house, it was still early. The girls were outside, doing the usual—smoking and texting. It reminded me of an old west saloon, where the harlots would line the edges of the balconies, displaying their plumage for all to see.

"Thanks," Combs said as we parked, "you ever been inside?"

"Nope," I replied, "Go ahead. I'll wait here."

"You have to come in with me and get this signed," he replied. After considering it, I guess I wasn't really that opposed to the idea. At least I'd get to know one secret before the day was over.

"Oh, right," I said, pretending I wasn't nervous. Combs opened his door first, tripped right out of the Jeep and fell flat on his face like a cousin. Dozens of papers flew out of the envelope. I leapt out of my seat and rounded the car to help him up. Several of the girls were watching from around the front yard.

"You alright?" I asked, collecting several photos that were quickly blowing away.

"Yeah," he replied, hoisting himself to his feet. He had managed to keep a hold on the book. He tried fruitlessly to wipe the grass stains from his Tiger Woods costume. I looked down and was stunned to see what I was holding. Among the loose papers and pictures from the envelope, there was a black and white photo of Kristy, standing next to her Camry.

"What's this?" I asked intently, not wanting to give away the fact that I knew her.

"Don't worry about it," Combs said, snatching the stack from my hands and stuffing them back inside the envelope. I looked around. The girls weren't paying attention any more. My blood was baked. I pulled out the gun and slammed my forearm against Combs' neck, pinning him to the Jeep with the gun stamping his cheek.

"You tell me what this is. Right now."

"New girls. You know that one?" he replied. I looked down at the photo in his hand, breathing heavily and then releasing his shirt.

"… No. Thought it was my sister for a second. Looked like her," I lied, looking around and putting the gun back at my waist. Combs laughed a little.

"That would suck," he joked. "Take it easy, alright? I'm sure this girl's around here somewhere. You can see for yourself" he added, putting things in order and walking towards the house. I followed him inside. It was just like you might imagine. It was really hot, there were skeezy people (guys and girls) sitting around the kitchen,

Nick May

a camera recording crew was setting up a few canopy lights and a tripod in the living room.

As we made our way down the long hallway past several closed rooms, it was quite audibly evident what was going on behind those doors. Either multiple people were giving birth in this house, or they were shooting no-no films. I just knew any second, I was going to see Kristy come out of one of those rooms wearing a headmaster's outfit or something. It would be more than I could stomach. Combs knocked on the door at the end of the hallway. All three of the doors behind us opened, revealing narrow portraits of odd things happening here and there. Those inside then returned to their duties upon realizing the knock wasn't for them. We waited patiently.

"Come in!" said someone on the other side. It was B's voice. Combs opened the door. I entirely expected to see B on her back with a camera in her face, but I was shocked to actually find her sitting on the floor (in her patented silk nighty), surrounded by toddlers with toys. It didn't phase Combs at all. He grabbed the W-9 out of my hand, added it to his stack and walked right over, bending down to trade papers with her. I remained at the doorway.

"Hey, John!" B said, signing various documents as Combs handed them to her.

"Hello," I sheepishly replied.

"You just missed all our noobs. They just left with Thom and his brothers and Deion. Bunch of hot new skanks," she said, retrieving a large envelope from the clinches of a slobbering two-year-old and handing it to Combs. "I'm just kidding. They're beautiful girls. We'll treat them well just like the rest." Combs took the wet envelope from B, grimacing.

"Was this girl with them?" he asked, showing B the photo of Kristy.

"Yeah, she's really sweet. Bit of a unique story, though," B replied.

"Where'd Thom take them?" I asked hastily.

"The beach," B replied.

"The motel?" I asked.

"Yeah," she said, bouncing one of the babies on her leg.

"Were they uh …?" I said, gesturing to the rooms.

"Oh, hell no. I wouldn't scare them off with this crap right away. Why are you so interested, John? Bored with Bobbie? She still not giving it up?" B joked bluntly.

"Nope. Not yet," I said, suddenly remembering Bobbie. "Shit!"

"Well don't be too frustrated, John. She's a lady," B replied. I didn't have time to kid around. Kristy was on her way to The Moss Head Motel and Bobbie was sitting on a curb somewhere. Look what I do to the women in my life. It had probably been half an hour easy. Combs was busy pushing papers, and I didn't have the patience to deal with another awkward car ride, so I bailed. Before I'd gotten to the front door, I'd dialed Kristy's number and had the phone to my ear. No answer. I looked at my screen and saw the nine missed calls from Bobbie.

When I got into the yard and looked up from my phone, I noticed that the green Rubicon had been overrun by an amateur adult film crew. There were big lights suspended around the Jeep, a camera on a tripod was poking in through the broken window, and there was a dude holding a boom mic through the driver-side door. I stood paused for a moment and watched as the Jeep rocked back and forth. This must have been the crew from the living room. They probably noticed my rolling set arrive and decided to switch locations for their flick.

"Hey!" I shouted. They all seemed to stop and look. "Out!" I yelled even louder as I pushed the boom kid out of the way and got in the driver side. It wasn't a surprise to see a naked couple in the back. The camera was still on and aimed right at me. "Get. Out," I said. That was enough for them. Within seconds, the Jeep was empty, but the smell remained. It was bad, to say the least. As I turned the key and yanked into reverse, I noticed Deion pulling into the driveway with a church van that said Justice Faith Tabernacle on the side. I was calling Kristy again. I watched as loads of new talent came pouring out of the van. Without blinking, I scoured every single face that came climbing out of the fifteen-passenger vessel—knowing any of them could be Kristy. I was relieved for the moment; however, Bobbie was going to be pissed. I gunned it.

Within moments, I was reaching over to open the door for Bobbie at the college.

"I'm so sorry!" I said, "Have you been waiting long?"

"About an hour and a half," she answered.

"An hour and a half?! What?!" I exclaimed, "Dammit, and I missed all your calls!"

"I called you like five minutes after I got done. I thought you were just circling the parking lot or something. Why did you leave?"

"I thought you were going to be a while. I'm so sorry!"

"John, why are you like sweating?" She looked at me, concerned. I peeled out.

"I had to go by Fran's, then take Combs to see B and it's just freaking so hot."

"Oooh. I see. That's fine. Yeah, I didn't know I'd be done that fast."

"So, you're not mad or anything?" I asked.

"No. You couldn't help it," she replied.

"I can't believe how awesome you are," I said. She smiled.

"I'm not awesome," she argued. "I'm just trying to stay on your good side."

"Why is that?" I asked.

"I like you, John," she said.

"I don't understand that," I insisted. "I haven't even gotten to turn my charm on yet. How can you already like me?"

"I liked you from the first night in the bed. It wasn't just that you showed an interest in me beyond sex. Lots of guys have done that, trying to rescue me and be my dad in shining armor."

"But, Bobbie, I asked you today if you ever wanted to give it up."

"Yeah, but you asked me in a way that showed some respect for my choices. I'm not stuck doing this, and you acknowledge that. So many guys have tried to just daddy me out of B's house. They would tell me it's for my own good. You think I want to be a career hooker?"

"What about the other night when I unsuccessfully tried to rescue you from Barry?"

"Well, John, I'm not going to deny the fact that we care about each other. I was getting that cock off your case, and you were trying, very valiantly, to get him off of mine. There's nothing wrong with that, and I never got to tell say thank you."

We parked back at the motel. It was getting dark and people were beginning to show up. Bobbie unbuckled, leaned in and started kissing my ear. I put my hand on her leg. My heart raced.

"So, you're sure you're not mad you had to wait for me?" I asked. Her lips moved down to my neck.

"John, I've already waited nineteen years for you," she said, turning my face to her lips. "What's another hour or so?" I felt her tongue. These kisses didn't feel performed like the first time. Not for me or for her. We kissed like that for several minutes, ranging from deep to light, each one locking me in even more than the last. She kissed her way back towards my ear. I faced forward, watching new girls trail in and out of the Winnebago.

"I think it's time to finish what we started," she whispered.

"Yep," I said, watching my ex-wife climb the stairs to her new office.

Book III

NATE

Minutemen

I still told people that Zwinny was my girlfriend, even though she was telling them that she wasn't. I've always believed we were made for each other. It seemed pretty obvious when we first started dating. She was the daughter of Dr. Darmin, a professor of religions at Emerald Breeze Junior College. My dad, Richard Flemington, was his boss and the dean. It just made sense to me then, but now that I think about it, those are the exact types of relationships that fail in America—the ones that make sense. Maybe it would have worked between us if we lived in a culture where marriages were arranged. I met Zwinny at the beginning of last summer when we were working on campus at the information desk in the Student Union. She was one year older than me and six inches taller. She had straight, black hair below her shoulders and wore things you might imagine a fortuneteller wearing. It had been a couple months since I'd seen her.

This is what she said to me the last time we saw each other:

"Nate, I want to see other people, or else I'll never know that we're right for each other."

"Ok. If that's what you think you have to do, I'll wait for you," I said.

"No, Nate," she protested. "You need to meet other people, too. What if you're wrong about me?"

"It's up to me, isn't it?" I asked.

"Yes, but I can't make any promises."

"I'm not asking you to."

"I can't tell you that I'll be back," she said. "I mean, I hope I will, but, you know, there may be someone else for me right around the corner." She was right. He was right around the corner. Literally. No, I mean, we were sitting at a Starbucks on 10th, and he was in the drive-thru when she walked out.

Apparently she had met him the night before at her friend, Karen's birthday party. That's what I hear. I decided to believe it was a coincidence. Here's a secret, however … that was not a coincidence. That's never a coincidence. I'll be blunt; if you don't allot at least one month for each year you dated your previous other before moving on to the new other, you've at least been spending some mental time in someone else's company (but I don't know this yet).

Several of my friends told me that I was in denial about what was happening with Zwinny. Regardless of how it looked, I was choosing to stay positive about the situation in hopes that she would be back. This was just a phase. Before long, she'd realize that she'd made a huge mistake, and that she wasn't going to be happy with anyone else but me. That was the whole point of this experiment that Zwinny was doing, wasn't it? She told me she had to do it in order to know if we were right for each other—not to know that we were wrong for each other.

"Bro, you're just sitting around in your room, waiting for her to come back. She's not coming back. She's long gone, man. It's time somebody gave you some tough love," my friends would say. They were dicks. I needed fans, not friends waiting in line to write me reality checks. I was quickly discovering that Zwinny had a method for dissolving relationships and cutting strings. It was like the way swarms of locusts treat crops. She would fly into a situation—a group of friends or a relationship—strip the subjects of what she needed for the time she needed it, and then she'd be long gone or dead before anyone would notice. That's what she was doing every single day—killing and dying. Locusts are older than high school juniors when they finally emerge in the killing fields. If Zwinny's mechanics were as close to a locust's as I thought they were, I could potentially be waiting a very long time.

Of course I asked myself, "why Zwinny?" In my head, most people climb a ladder to get to the roof—one rung at a time. I was born on the roof. That's where I met Zwinny. I was making the climb down because it was the only direction to go from there.

"You've got a pretty low view of yourself," my parents would say. Yes, mom. I do. For the rest of my life, Zwinny Darmin—the epitome of female minds, is dumping me one day at a time. That was "why Zwinny …" She had a body that every male she came into contact with would mentally undress, but it was her soul that I latched onto. Most people couldn't understand why they were infatuated with Zwinny's personality. I honestly didn't know why, either. Maybe later I'd realize that she, like millions of others, was just a cool person. Nothing more.

This guy she had been hanging out with for the last few months (the one she subsequently met at a party just before dumping me and meeting him again five minutes later), well I Facebook stalked the shit out of him. I actually created a fake profile for a Marco Buttermore with the sole purpose of creeping on him and Zwinny. I missed the part where she changed her relationship status to single after she stopped seeing me, so I avoided the hurt that could have potentially wrought, but I was sticking a potato peeler into my heart every day, anyway, looking at their pages, waiting for new photos to show up with the two of them

71

together or for that status to change, igniting my humiliation.

Are people aware of the embarrassment that comes from changing relationship statuses on Facebook? It's such a public thing. It's like asking someone to marry you on the big screen at an NBA game, but instead, The LEDs say, "Nate Flemmington just got dumped." You know how when starting a relationship on Facebook, both parties have to agree? I think it would be funny if both parties had to agree to disagree when breaking up on Facebook. The whole world would just be locked in this confusing tug-of-war with one side of the relationship saying, "It's over! Let me date this other person!" and the other side saying, "Oh, no it's not!" Maybe you'd have to open a ticket with Facebook support in order to break up with someone. It would be like a virtual dating court.

I was only with Zwinny for three months, and I had tons of people posting on my Wall, asking what was up or if I was ok. Some people even assumed we were still together (apparently missing the news) and would be shocked once they noticed. These were the people who would come up to me, prior to noticing, and say, "hey, dude! How are things with Zwinny?" and I'd say, "They're good, man ... where have you been—trapped in a mine?"

I actually saw him a lot—Zwinny's new interest. I almost quit my fast food job because of the sheer amount of times he would visit. He'd order a number one with a Coke every single time. What an adventurous spirit. He'd eat that thing plain, too. There was nothing harder for me to understand than people who ate things without sauce. Half the reason I got anything anywhere was so I could dip it in some sauce.

We invented chicken nuggets so we'd have something to put barbecue on. He must have worked for the Sherriff's Office because he was always wearing dress clothes and some sort of badge, and he always carried handcuffs. He never seemed to have any clue who I was. Zwinny must have never mentioned me. That was typical for a locust. This guy was huge. I could wear him as a suit and drive him around. I never did anything to his food (though several of my friends did after I explained to them who he was). Many of them tried to dig up dirt on him for me but were unsuccessful. No one knew where he was from. He sort of just showed up one day. This gave me a good excuse to seek more serious means for exposing him.

This is when I kicked into super stalker mode. I knew I was probably doing the wrong thing. I knew I probably should have been concerned with showing Zwinny what she was missing, but I was more preoccupied with showing Zwinny what she was getting. Most of my logical friends and family told me that I should just chill out, be normal and be confident. I knew they were right because the more I ignored her, the more she texted me to see how I was doing. Despite this truth, I kept denying the science and went about trying to pin something on the guy. I'd follow him around cyberspace, looking for questionable pictures or notes that I could tag Zwinny in so she'd see them. When that didn't work, I started following him around town. This was my "future wife" he was messing with. I was going to bust him hard.

During the day, his course seemed pretty inconsequential. He'd leave his house down by the marina around 7 A.M. and would spend most of his day at the station. He'd usually only leave for lunch or the occasional trip across the bridge to the beach (which I assumed was to sneak some alone time with Zwinny during the later part of the day). I didn't cross the bridge. There was this weird finality about it. Number one: I didn't want to see them together for real. Number two: I just didn't like crossing the bridge. It felt like I was driving so far. Half the time, I'd end up just staking out down at the east end, waiting for him to come back across. I know this is starting to sound crazy, but listen, when you love someone, there's crazy, then actions cease to be crazy and they become necessary. You'll tell yourself anything in the world to retain your sanity. She was the one who was unknowingly hurting herself. I was going to prove that to her.

He started going to her house more and more frequently throughout the following days. My word, at the very least, I could get him fired for neglecting his work. Maybe Zwinny would be less attracted to an unemployed man. That wouldn't work. They'd know that someone had followed them. Fingers would point to me. This sucked. Every day, I'd stop at this park just before the bridge and feel completely idiotic for not having the balls to commit to my pursuit.

I had basically memorized his schedule, and because his visits to the beach had become so regular, I had stopped following him so tediously, and I would more or less just check certain places at certain times of the day to make sure he was there. This guy relived the same day over and over and over. Freaking Bill Murray. I suppose one could say the same of me. I had done nothing more than creep this guy for the last straight week. I was sitting at the park on a Friday evening, waiting for his undercover police Charger to come growling by on his way across the bridge. He was running way later than usual. I'd thought about trying to find him, but I couldn't go snooping around town at this time of day. He was off work already and God only knew where he was now.

The sun had almost gone down when I finally saw the grey muscle car pull up to the stop light just before the bridge. I sat there biting my nails with the engine running. Something was different about tonight. His abnormal schedule had my senses heightened. I was curious as to where he'd been and how Zwinny would react to him being so late for their daily appointment. Part of me needed to see this. This was the closest I'd been, mentally, to following him any further. I felt like their mood or their emotions were taking a deeper dive, and I wasn't going to be there to police it unless I adapted. What if they were in love? What if there relationship was moving out of this rigid, daytime lunch date feel to a more frivolous, romantic, candlelit dinner stage? I sure as hell wasn't going to let that happen.

The light turned green, and for the seventh time since I'd begun this little venture, he started off across the bridge. I took my hand out of my mouth and looked at my phone. Six o' clock. I could see the Charger disappearing over the bay. "What are you doing, man? Just follow him!" I thought to myself. I saw the trail of red taillights leading me to absolution. Without another second's hesitation, I rolled out and cut my way into traffic, rolling down the windows to let in the night air. I was close behind.

Within seconds, I was over the bridge and wheeling down onto the beach roads. It really wasn't so bad once I was over. Maybe it truly was the water I was afraid of. I'd had nightmares about strange bridges with frightening procedures for crossing them. One of them was a real long sucker that stood about a foot high and cut through a marshy bay. At a certain point, the bridge would make a ninety-degree vertical angle that went straight up about a hundred feet. My vehicle would have to pick up enough speed to fly off the end, do a back flip and land vertically going down the bridge's opposite, identical side. I don't know what the purpose of a bridge with a function like that would serve, but it scared the shit out of me.

I didn't know anything on the beach. The only path I'd ever taken was straight to Zwinny's, and I'd even avoided that one in every instance that I could. He seemed to be sticking to it, though. I guess I was right. He was headed to her house. The traffic was bad at this time of the evening near the beginning of the weekend. The gulf roads were filled with clubbers and leftover tourists, and there were floods of people walking everywhere. It was right then that I noticed Karen, Zwinny's friend strolling amongst the crowds down the Beachside Walk with a group of girls. With a shock and a sting in my heart, I immediately noticed Zwinny walking beside her. It was weird that I hadn't noticed her first. Why was the world so small? Traffic was crawling. Within seconds I'd be less than three feet away from them, and they would have to be blind not to see me. I tried my best to hide, leaning forward and looking in the opposite direction, but embarrassment has a way of finding us—the way you'll be in class and go to pick that razorback that's taxing the roof of your right nostril just as the thong girl you sit behind turns to ask you for a pencil.

"Nate!" she yelled. I turned quickly, acting overly surprised. I waved and mouthed something, pointing ahead. What an idiot. The windows were open and I was mouthing things. She looked good. She looked happy. Someone honked. I faced forward. The light was go, and the Charger was nowhere to be seen. I quickly closed the gap between the next car and me, forgetting about Zwinny. Where did he go?! I scanned the area and suddenly noticed the Charger heading up Scotland. I recognized the taillights. I was doing my best to get up behind him again when my phone rang. Zwinny. Of course.

"Hey!" I answered. I was panicked and losing him.

"Hey! What are you doing over here?" she asked. "You never come to the beach."

"Yeah, I'm … well, I'm … I'm going to this … I had to run to the beach store to get cups." I was doing my best to keep up with the Charger. We weren't going to Zwinny's, and it seemed as if she wasn't expecting company, considering she wasn't home.

"Oh. Ok. Well, I was just calling to say hi," she said. "I saw you and just thought I'd see what was up. Have a good night!"

"You, too." I hung up. I was experimenting with the idea of treating Zwinny like she was the last thing on Earth that I was concerned with. I needed to make it appear like I was a confident, independent man with an agenda, even though I knew I was far from.

Without as much as a blinker, the Charger yanked into some obscure parking lot before I could even tell what it was. I kept on driving, attempting to stay as inconspicuous as possible. I looked in my rearview to see where he might have gone, but only observed neon lights and the Beachside Walk as far as the eye could see. By the time I made my way back around, I'd forgotten just how far back he'd dipped in. The first place I was able to turn into was this run-down motel with two or three tour busses parked together in the front. It was packed. Who in their right mind would want to stay in a place like this? Nearly every door was open, the trashiest of the trashy slithered about, and there wasn't a parking spot in site. The lot was centered around a dried-up old pool or garden by the looks of it. I slowly made my way around, hoping to catch site of him. I couldn't believe how crazy the place was. There were clubs down on this end of the beach that looked less happening than this motel. There were so many people that I could barely inch my car across the gravel.

No one seemed to notice me. There were so many cars coming and going that I was finally able to find a spot around back. There were things going on back there that I don't even want to begin to speculate. I got out and locked the door, looking around. There were several dark figures here and there. A couple people were hunched down between two cars doing something with a coat hanger. The better part of me assumed that they were just breaking into a locked car. I walked off towards the light of the parking lot. A girl screamed. I kept walking. There were groups of people gathered all over the place, and there were ten different kinds of loud music coming from thirty separate directions. People were yelling and howling. Scantily clad women walked here and there. I know I at least smelled pot, among other things. People circulated through rooms like blood through the chambers of a heart.

I walked about casually, keeping my eyes open for the Charger or its driver, half expecting to smell cotton candy or see a clown with balloons. This had to be where he stopped. People awkwardly stood in what seemed to be lines, awaiting entry to rooms or to some bits of activity taking place at various hubs around the lot. I guess I could most closely relate it to a carnival or bazaar of some kind. Suddenly, I saw it. The grey car sat parked right up front. I must have missed it when I drove in. My eyes widened as I shrunk back behind a bus, still searching the crowds for his face. He was here. The good news was that I could guarantee at least something happening here was illegal. If I could lay eyes on him, I will have finally caught him red-handed.

I had an idea. Zwinny had just seen me on the beach. As far as she was concerned, I was on my way somewhere when my car ran out of gas and I was forced to call her because she was the only person I could think of. All I needed to do was get Zwinny to the motel, accidentally let her see him partaking in some sort of shady activity and then be there to pick up the pieces. Brilliant. I needed to locate the guy first. I waited several more minutes and then finally spotted him skipping a line and breezing right into one of the rooms that, upon closer inspection, looked like it was hosting some sort of drunken, nude art show. All I saw were bottles, boobs and body paint.

I quickly made my way back to the side of the motel. I kept my distance from the makeshift abortion clinic or whatever the hell was going on back there where my car was parked and I was too afraid to go. The noise was at least a little muffled over here. Without thinking, I dialed Zwinny. It rang. She picked up.

"Hello?"

"Hey, Zwinny," I swallowed. "Sorry. Are you busy?"

"Um, I'm just sitting up at Banger Grill. What's up?" she asked genuinely.

"Well, I feel bad about this, but, I sort of ran out of gas and coasted into this really seedy motel or something, and you were the only person I could think of to call, but if you're eating, I can try to get someone else to come get me or bring me some gas or something."

"Um, are you sure?" she asked hesitantly. Crap, she's supposed to insist.

"Yeah, well are you close? Let's see, Banger Grill?" I replied, piling on the pressure.

"No, Nate, it's fine. We'll come over there. I think I know what place you're talking about. I think we passed it earlier."

"Ah, man … are you sure?" I pretended. "Thanks so much. I hate to bother you."

"It's no problem. I'll call you when we get there so you can tell us where you are."

"Ok. Thanks so much!" I said.

"No prob. See you in a minute."

Ok. I was set. I'd get Zwinny to come around back where I'd hop in her car with her and tell her to drive around front so I could let the owner know I'd be leaving the car overnight. I'd put her in plain site of the room and hope to God that she saw him in there messing around with some girl or something. Maybe she'd at least see his car and make up the rest. Not to mention, this was going to give me some time to pull the nostalgia card and talk about the good ole days (which were like a couple months ago). I stood around the corner, spying out the room from across the lot. It was getting more and more packed which meant it would be getting harder for Zwinny to discover him inside doing something unfaithful. She better hurry. My phone rang.

"Hey," I answered.

"Hey, this is crazy! Where are you?" she asked.

"I'm in the back."

"In the back? How did you—hold on." I could hear the girls talking amongst themselves, but I couldn't tell what they were saying. I spotted Zwinny's car halted in front of the very room that he was in. With my ear still to the phone, I could hear several girls' voices and then suddenly, Zwinny's broke through,

"That better not be him," she said. "Nate, I'll call you back in just a second." She hung up the phone. I froze. My eyes were fixed on her. She'd seen him. It worked. I stood there and watched as she jumped out of the car, leaving it running with her friends still sitting inside in the middle of the busy parking lot. This was almost too perfect.

A couple minutes passed. Karen climbed into the front seat. The car finally began to move again. The girls had started towards me when we all noticed Zwinny stomping forth from the crowd, angrily dragging what's his face to a clear spot near the pool. Karen inched Zwinny's car slowly towards back. I waved them down. She rolled down the window as I put my hand on the roof and leaned over.

"Where's Zwinny?" I pretended.   Someone screamed.

"Um ..." Karen looked back, "She's dealing with something."

"Oh," I pretended. Again. I watched from afar as Zwinny seemed to be giving him the lecture of a lifetime. There were lots of arms flying around, hand gestures and extreme facial expressions. Brilliant. She'd blast something at him, and he'd say something calmly back, motioning this way and that, but then, to my dismay, the air began to change. I couldn't believe what I saw next. She put her hand over her mouth, holding back laughter. He smiled. They hugged and then kissed. What the hell, man! I looked into the car. The girls were as shocked as I was, though I pretended not to notice.

Before long, Zwinny was walking over. I faked like I was gathering things from my car. Honestly, it was going to be a huge inconvenience to leave my car there overnight just to stay true to my charade. I had counted on spending the night with Zwinny and being her revenge. Now I had to think of something quick to avoid an awkward-ass car ride and the hassle of coming back in the morning. With my back turned, I listened as she laughingly explained to the girls what was going on.

"He's doing an investigation," she whispered.

"What?!" The girls replied. "Really?!"

"Yeah, apparently there is a lot of bad stuff happening here," she laughed. "We need to leave as soon as possible." She turned to me, "Hey Nate!" She came over and gave me a hug. I was holding some worthless pile of possessions. If she would have noticed I had a dirty sock and a bag of trash in my hand, I would have felt really dumb. "How are you?" she asked. Someone screamed again.

"I'm good. Thanks for doing this. Did you get stopped up over there, or?" I asked, trying desperately to get her to spill.

"Oh, yeah," she looked back. "It's nothing. Saw someone I knew." I glanced at the car. The girls were being awkward. "So, what's going on over there?" Zwinny motioned in the opposite direction. I looked.

There was a guy sitting alone at an overturned cable spool with some light emanating from the middle

"Yeah. I don't know," I said, annoyed. "We should probably go."

"Yeah, definitely," Zwinny agreed. I locked and closed my doors and walked around to the passenger side of her car. Karen and the other two girls had crammed into the backseat and were waiting silently.

"Thanks again for doing this. I really appreciate it," I said as I settled into the front seat.

"You're welcome. Do you want to go to a gas station, or do you want us to just drop you off in town?" Zwinny asked, pulling down a dirt side road that exited the rear of the motel.

"Oh! Yeah, a gas station would be great. I hadn't really considered that option. I'm an idiot. Do you have a gas can?" I asked.

"Nope." Zwinny replied. Great. I was going to have to buy a can and fill it with gas to bring back and put in my car that's sitting in some scary-ass motel with a full tank already.

"That's cool. I need to get one anyway," I lied.

The car ride was dead silent for the remainder of the short trip. So much for nostalgia. The girls were awkward because they knew what had just happened. They didn't really know me that well, and I could tell they were already more on the other guy's team than mine. I felt so out of place for what seemed like an eternity. We had to go five minutes out of the way to find "gulf-friendly" gas because Zwinny didn't want to support the BP that was right around the corner from the motel. As we pulled into some sketchy gas station, Zwinny answered a phone call. It was him. I got out of the car without saying a word and went inside to continue the act. The clerk was Middle-Eastern—no older than me.

"How can I help you today, sir?" he said from behind the counter, standing in front of a rack of porn. I paused and looked around. This was essentially a sex shop that sold gas.

"I just need to get a gas can and I need to put ten in it," I said.

"Very good, sir. All the gas cans are right behind you on the bottom shelf." I turned and noticed the giant, red containers sitting snuggly between a stack of boxed blow-up dolls and a crate of rubber body parts. I threw the money on the counter, got my change and walked towards the car. Zwinny was smiling—still on the phone. I begrudgingly pumped the unnecessary gas into the unnecessary tank and got back in the car, placing the red container on the floor between my feet. Zwinny was embarrassingly trying to get off the phone as fast as possible.

"Ok. I'll talk to you later."

Silence.

"You, too …"

Annoyed.

"… I love you, too."

Knives.

"Sorry," she said, "Didn't know I'd be on that long." I didn't say anything. I just couldn't believe what an awkward situation I'd gotten myself into. I was beginning to realize how ridiculous I'd been acting. I was a case, for sure. The ride back ended up being just like the ride from, and before long, we were re-parking in the darkened backdrop of the motel.

"Thanks," I said, trying to sound relieved, "you saved my life."

"You're welcome. Be safe," she said, reaching in for a hug. As we came in close, something on Zwinny's hand gashed my arm. I made a saliva-sucking sound and reeled back. "Oh! I'm sorry! Did I get you?!" I looked at my arm. There was a red stripe scoring my bicep.

"Ah, what was that?" I said as the pain deadened. Zwinny was looking at her fingers, and then I saw it, glinting like a damn crystal cathedral. She hesitated, holding up her hand.

"It must have been my uh ..." I stared at the rock on her finger that had said everything she couldn't. The physical scar caused by the ring would prove to be no match against the emotional one it would undoubtedly leave behind.

"Bye," I said, quickly exiting the car and grabbing the jug of irrelevant gas. As Zwinny drove off, I noticed that the back lot had emptied (except for the gentleman at the glowing table who had now been joined by several other figures) and that my car now sat on four neat stacks of bricks. I had been gone maybe ten minutes. Was this a joke? My immediate thought was to inform the motel staff, but then I quickly realized that they probably weren't the most upstanding people, either. Hell, it was probably them who took my tires (and I sure as hell wasn't going to ask the drug-induced seance what happened to my tires). It was getting late—late for me at least. The fact that my vehicle was now a permanent decoration at this strange motel was amongst the least of my thoughts. My girlfriend was engaged to another man.

I decided to stroll around front again to see if there was anyone that could help me out. To tell you the truth, I really didn't care what happened at that point.

I didn't want to take a cab to my place or father Dick's house, and I didn't feel like being with friends who were only going to tell me they told me so. The party was still as lively as ever, only the busses were missing. I made my way across the white gravel to what seemed the most like an office. The door was wide open. Next door was a room-full of guys administering what looked like measured doses of heroin from needles while patients sat bracing in patio furniture. The office was empty, but I could tell someone had just been there because of the half-finished game of Minesweeper on the PC monitor behind the desk. Just then, a young guy walked in, gave me a casual salute and went behind the counter to a pot of coffee.

"Hey," I started, "I was wondering if there are any rooms available?" He turned around with a full cup in his hand and took a sip of the hot beverage, leaning back against the desk on the opposite wall. He smiled.

"Ah, whadya got, like human torture for money? You one of those dudes who steals girls from Disney cruises and sells their bodies?" He took another sip. I looked down at myself and then back up at him, puzzled.

"No …?" I replied.

"Eh, I always figured that was next," he said.

"Um, I parked my car around back—"

"Yikes, bad move," he interrupted.

"Yeah … someone stole my tires."

"Yeah, the Bean Bag Brothers are branching out a bit into looting and such. Sorry, man."

"So you know who took them?" I asked.

"Yeah. Well," he took a sip, "maybe, but I can't get them back. They're long gone."

"Oh … well, can you tell me who it was so I can ask them?"

"Do you want to get your ass kicked and have your wallet stolen, too?" He stared at me. I sighed.

"Can you just rent me a room? I just need to sleep. No torture," I said, taking out my wallet.

"Actually, I don't technically work here. I work for the RV, but I can tell you there aren't any rooms available at the moment. Your best bet for getting a bed tonight is paying for a girl."

"A girl?" I held my wallet open, staring at the stranger.

"Yeah," he took a sip.

"You mean, like a prostitute?" I asked. He nodded. "Oh, I don't have money for that."

"Yeah, well, suit yourself," he replied. I sat there weighing the options. Which choice would be more shameful: explaining myself to my ride or sharing a bed with a stranger?

"What's the cheapest one?" I asked. He laughed a bit.

"Actually, I've got some new ones that we're still working with—if you're interested in amateurs. I'll get you one of those for a regular room price."

"That's fine. I'm not looking to sleep with any of them," I said.

"Oh, right," he said, nodding his head, like he was just going along with an act.

"All I have is a card, though," I added.

"Here, hand it to me," he said, putting his coffee down and taking my card to the computer, "Technically, we've got a bill here, so I'll just swipe you on the motel system and deduct that from what we owe."

"So this place is like a flea market for misdemeanor vendors?" I asked.

"Straight-edge, homes," he said, tearing off my receipt and handing it to me with my card.

"What does that mean?" I asked.

"Upstairs," he ignored me. "201. Girl's name is Kristy. She'll let you in. I'll call up."

"Thanks," I said, putting my wallet away. He smiled and nodded with his ear to the phone.

I'd spend the night here and sort something out in the morning. I wasn't the kind of guy who trusted public transit, I refused to tell anyone about this and my car was on blocks, so this was my only option. I climbed the office-side stairs to the second floor. 201 was the first room. I looked around to make sure no one was spying on me—like it would matter if they were. No one here had any clue who I was. I rapped lightly. Several seconds later, a skinny girl with a short, blonde wife-cut opened the door. She didn't seem very warm, but she was also cleaner than I'd expected. She looked like she'd been ripped right out of a Christian sitcom about a middle-class family.

"Hello," I said, smiling. She didn't say a word. She just left the door open and walked back into the room. I could tell she was exhausted. She was about to get a surprise. I bolted the door and sat down on the foot of the bed. "Kristy, right?" I asked, taking off my shoes.

"Yes," she replied. She was hovering around in between the bathroom and the vanity.

"Listen, I'm literally just paying for this room so I can sleep. I don't care about anything else. I've got stolen tires, a broken heart and I'm just tired. You ok with that?" She paused and looked at me.

"What?" She seemed stunned.

"Take the night off. I'm not interested in soliciting you. I just want to think through some things, come up with my next plan of action and then sleep." She stood still. What happened next, I can't begin to understand. She started to cry.

"Woah! I'm not trying to offend you! There were just no other rooms available." I got up and walked towards her. She recoiled, sniffling.

"No, it's not that," she protested. "I'm just tired, too."

"You're crying because you're tired?" I touched her elbow. She immediately turned and embraced me with everything she had. What the hell kind of hooker was this? She just kept saying, "Thank you," and wouldn't let go of my neck. We stood there for three or four minutes before she finally let go and went and curled up on the bed without even getting under the covers. She looked like a little girl who had no clue where she was. I stood there, staring at her. This was the weirdest night of my life.

"You know, the guy down in the office, he seemed pretty cool. Is he your boss?" I asked. "If you don't like what you're doing, I'm sure he'd—"

"Who, Thom? No, it's not that. It's just this whole situation, I never thought I'd find myself here," she sniffed. "I'm grateful to be out of the place where I was."

"Where was that?" I asked, sitting down on the other side of the bed. It was nice to get my mind onto someone else's sick excuse for a life. She rolled over and looked at me. Her eyes were red and puffy. The corners of her mouth were wet, like she'd been drooling.

89

"… You're really not here to sleep with me?" she asked.

"No. I promise. I'm don't really solicit prost—like … girls. I've got my own baggage," I stumbled. The room went silent for a couple minutes. Kristy looked up at the sparkly ceiling.

"… I was married and on my way to becoming a mother. I started to get the feeling that things weren't working with my husband, so I left him. A few months later, I was in a bathroom at the mall food court.… I thought I had a stomach ache, so I went to the bathroom. Five minutes later I was …" she began to cry even harder this time. "… I was fishing it out of the water …" I stared at her, waiting for whatever came next. She continued. "The thought of flushing it scared me so much, so I just left it on the seat." She was now full-on weeping. I couldn't believe the story that was coming out of her mouth.

"To make a long story short, I met a guy who said he'd make me forget about all that. He was this real cute guy; nice car, place on the water. Well, my parents didn't agree with me seeing him so soon after my divorce and the trauma of losing my child. They also just didn't like him. Said they could tell he was bad news. I don't even care that they were right this one time!" she argued. "They'd said the same thing about every guy I'd ever liked. The one time in my life that they were right, and they expect me to believe they have some keen sense for sniffing out bad guys. Give me a break. They hated my ex-husband back when we were dating, until he started making money. The point is, if I was wrong, they'd say they warned me. If I was right, they'd say, 'you're welcome.' I was tired of all that."

"They said they wouldn't talk to me as long as I continued to see him, so naturally, I just wanted to do anything I could to oppose them at that point. I did everything in my ability to make it work. Pretty soon, he started hitting me and forcing me to sleep with him, even though I told him I didn't want to. Before long, I realized what he really was. Within a month, he was pimping me out to whomever, whenever. If I refused, he'd just beat me more. That's the tame version. The other version involves chains ... That's when Deion came and brought me to Thom and B. I just needed protection, you know? I always criticized women for not just leaving situations like that, but until you're in it yourself, you can't possibly hope to understand. I've never been so scared in my entire life."

"So did this Thom guy help you?" I asked, sitting frozen on the bed.

"Well, he said the only way they could guarantee that I'd be safe was if I came and worked for them. They said they'd dealt with this guy before, and those girls were doing fine now. At that point, I would have taken any way out. It was a deal that I was more than willing to make. I knew that neither my parents nor anyone else would ever look at me again.

"You'd have to understand the tribe I come from; our beliefs—which really have nothing to do with how my parents act. I'd much rather be this person than let my parents live for me until I meet someone they can marry. I'm not going to make life choices for them, and I refuse to reach this harmony one day where we're both content with the same man. That's not a solution. Maybe it's terrible to say, but the last thing I want is for my parents to be happy with my decisions. It's the only way I know I'm in control."

"Did they catch this guy and deal with him?" I asked.

"No," she answered. "They beat up a man they thought was him, but it was actually just someone who worked for him."

"Have you talked to your ex-husband?" I asked. "Surely you know someone who won't judge you …"

"I can't depend on that. If I feel any sort of shame, it's in front of him. At the same time, I made a decision, and I can't——"

——Suddenly, the motel room door was kicked in before Kristy could utter another word. Kristy and I both jumped. She grabbed onto my hand as a tall guy with a wife beater and a half-zipped hazmat suit entered the room. His hair was in a long, greasy ponytail. He swung the door closed as Kristy and I sat up in the bed with confused and scared expressions across our faces.

"I knew you were here," he said. "Saw that Jeep of yours I put a couple holes in." He stalked up and down in front of the bed.

"I'm sorry, you must think I'm someone else." I said, surrendering my hands and standing up.

"No. I know exactly who you are. You've been sleeping with my wife, and then she sends you to my house to take our son!"

"What?!" I asked, completely baffled. Kristy jumped in.

"Sir, are you sure you have the right room?"

"You better shut that bitch up if you know what's good for her," he demanded. Kristy and I looked at each other, knowing we were dealing with a lunatic. "First, you're gonna tell me where B is, and then, you and I are gonna settle the score."

"Listen …" I said, standing to my feet in front the greasy giant. "I don't know who B is, and I don't have

92

a score to settle with you or your son," I probably shouldn't have gotten that brave. As a response to my boldness, the crazed intruder produced a huge knife. I only caught a glimpse of it. It was black and green with tons of jagged edges and random holes in the blade—like the ones you see at flea markets. The next thing I knew, I went completely numb as the butt of the knife went straight to my skull. Kristy screamed from the bed. It was the worst thing I had ever heard—the sound combination of the knife hilt smacking my bone and Kristy's blood-boiling screams, unleashing hell on my ears.

The next twenty minutes or so were very interesting. It seemed to be that I was hovering above the room, looking down on my assaulter, my unconscious body lying there on the floor and Kristy, still screaming from the bed. I could hear people running up the stairs just outside the room. The giant quickly grabbed Kristy and yanked her off the bed. Her screams only became louder with more clearly-formed words, only I couldn't tell what they were. He positioned himself behind her near the bathroom, his forearm bracing her neck, holding the knife to her throat. Within seconds, the guy from the office, whose name was Thom, according to Kristy, came slamming through the door with a guy I hadn't seen yet. They both had guns drawn and aimed straight at the intruder. The one I didn't know yelled,

"Kris, you ok?! Did he hurt you?!" She was crying so uncontrollably that her vocal chords couldn't even catch. Her eyes were closed as she mouthed something like, "No. Please help, God." I couldn't tell. Thom was on the floor now checking for my pulse. He was feeling in the wrong place.

"Let go of her you asshole!" said the other one.

"John!" Kristy screamed. Thom looked up, pointing his gun.

"Joel, let her go, man! She didn't do anything! It's me you want, right?" He pointed to his bruised eye. "Remember?" Joel looked down at my body on the floor, clearly realizing that he had indeed made a mistake. A small crowd was starting to form on the stairs just outside the door, but there were two other guys outside near the rail holding them back.

"Look, I'm gonna slowly make my way out of here," Joel said, rotating through the room, past my body in a slow dance with John and Thom, still clinching Kristy and holding the knife to her neck. All sound escaped the room except for soft, careful footsteps. "I'm gonna be back for you, buddy. I promise!" Joel said, gesturing towards Thom as he stepped in front of the open door.

"That's fine, dude. Just let her go," Thom said. I could see that John's eyes were watering a little as he kept the gun aimed so close to Kristy's head. He must've known her closely. I kept glancing back at myself to see if I was ok. I clearly wasn't. I hadn't moved. Just then, a new figure appeared in the doorway behind Joel. It was him—Zwinny's fiancé. I never thought I'd be the least bit happy to see that guy. We all noticed him at once. He kicked Joel hard in the side. Kristy was released.

"Freeze!" he screamed, but Joel didn't listen. He turned and surprised everyone, catching Zwinny's fiancé right between his shoulder and neck with that serrated blade. Kristy fainted and fell to the floor as John fired seven rounds into Joel. Both Joel and his victim collapsed on the floor, bracing their wounds as blood spilt all over the brown carpet.

Thom leapt over the bodies that lay on the floor, saying something to the guys outside and closing the door the best he could. It sounded as if the small group outside had quickly dispersed and gone about their business once they heard the shots. I should've known this place wasn't really the type to show much concern over things like screaming women and gunshots. I hope they were just afraid. Was this hell? Had the bridge really collapsed on my way over, and had I drowned in the warm bay water, sinking to the depths inside my car? I felt my hearing and vision slowly begin to fade.

Thom began spewing out orders. He and John lifted my body into the bed. They left Joel and Kristy lying on the floor and carried Zwinny's fiancé to the door. His eyes were still open, and he was saying something in between growls and heavy breaths. Thom and John opened the door and handed him over—knife still protruding from his neck region—to the two guys outside and then came back inside the room, closing the door once again. As my vision and hearing decayed even more, I saw John bent down over Kristy. Thom stood over our bodies. Their mouths were moving, but they were completely silent as I drifted away into blackness.

I retained my thought process as my vision faded. Joel was dead, but I was pretty sure I wasn't. I found myself walking in utter darkness. Every few minutes, a tiny blinking light would appear above my head. I couldn't tell if they were very close or very far away like stars. Though these lights kept appearing one by one, I was still unable to see my feet or what kind of surface I was walking on. I bent down—still moving—to run the tips of my fingers along the ground. It felt like asphalt—gritty and warm.

I walked for what seemed like hours. By now, the air above me was filled with thousands of tiny lights, and things around and before me began to materialize. I could only see what light the small stars reflected off of various surfaces. I could see light in the contour of a tree, but no tree. I could see light that formed the edges of a fence, but no fence. I could see billions of shimmering drops of dew on the ground, on what must have been wet grass, but I couldn't make out the individual blades. There was something great about it. It reminded me most of that unusual paper that you get in art class as a child. You etch away the surface with a tool of some kind, revealing the brightly colored pallet beneath. I kept walking. I'd noticed the further I walked, the more light would encompass the world around me, rendering things even more detailed.

As I walked even further, and more and more light was shed from this unknown source, colors began to appear on the surface of things. I was soon able to make out the entire shape of the fence that I was walking beside. The asphalt had turned to dark green grass beneath my shoes, and a bright and colorful park had appeared in front of me. There was no sun, but the light on everything was as bright as it would have been during the day. It was then that I truly realized that vision is solely based on the amount of light that interacts with the surfaces of things. Sure, it seems like a pretty simple idea now, but one would have had to see what I saw in order to truly grasp the revelation that had befallen me at that exact moment between two worlds.

As I walked closer to the park, I realized it was situated in an urban environment that was unfamiliar to me. There were tall buildings all around whose exteriors reflected the light of a hidden sun, though the sky far above them was as dark as space. I heard someone whispering what seemed to be my name through the squeaking of the swing set—that sound that when mixed with the blood smell of iron chains, can all at once cause a person to feel overrun with nausea. Even as I stared at the empty swing, moving back and fourth beneath the candy-striped bars, she sat there—like she had been there all along—a thin, pale girl in ordinary clothes. She had brown hair. Her eyes—a color I knew but could not remember—navigated my face. I was unknown to her. Her feet met the worn dirt beneath the swing, as we both stopped before each other.

"Hello," she said.

"Hi," I replied. "Did you say my name?"

No," she said.

"Where are we?" I asked.

"I'm not sure really," she answered. "What's the last thing you remember?"

"Oh, I remember everything. My actual body is lying unconscious on a motel room floor right now. A guy named Joel hit me."

"Oh. Yeah, it's all starting to make sense," she said, standing from the swing.

"What do you mean?" I asked.

"Well, the last thing I remember, I was driving really fast on a busy road. It was pretty dark. As the headlights flew past my car, I started to imagine how the slightest touch of the wheel could kill me. I'm not psychotic or anything, but I kept imagining the scenario over and over in my head."

"Well, it looks like you may have done it," I laughed.

"Isn't that weird?" she asked. "My imagination was making it so real in my head, that any one of those times could have been the one where I yanked my car over."

"So, are you dead?" I asked, looking around.

"I'm pretty sure," she replied.

"Maybe I'm dead, too then," I said. "It definitely doesn't feel like it."

"Can you still see anything at the motel?" she asked me.

"No, not at all. Can you see anything where you came from?"

"Yeah, everything," she replied, walking to a bench and sitting down. I followed her. "That's basically how I know I'm dead."

"So there's obviously some differences between our situations. That's for sure."

"Yeah, maybe," she replied, "Joel's bark is bigger than his bite. You're not dead."

"He stabbed a guy in the neck!" I argued. "Wait, do you know Joel?"

"I can see everything that's going on at that motel," she said.

"What?" I asked, sitting down beside her.

"I was watching my sister at first. She's there."

"Kristy? Is Kristy your sister?" I asked.

"No," she said.

"Oh," I replied. We sat in silence for a while. I looked around at the buildings surrounding the park. "Are you able to see what's going on where I am right now?" I asked.

"Yep, everything that's happened since you showed up," she replied.

"Really?! What's happening?"

"Nothing," she answered. "You and Joel are side by side on the bed. He's dead. You're sleeping. Thom and John gave the cop guy to some kids I don't know. They took him back to Indian River." I was reminded of Zwinny.

"Does Zwinny know?" I asked.

"No, but I assume she's getting worried now. Why are you there, anyway, Nate?" She wondered.

"How do you know my name?" I demanded. "I thought you hadn't seen me until now."

"Oh, well, it's Kristy. She's back in the room, and she's saying your name," the girl replied. I sat quietly. I could hear her clearly now; whispering. It was definitely Kristy's voice ringing in my ears. "Were you following him or something?" the girl asked bluntly.

"No!" I bit back. "Dammit, I'm so confused! How long am I going to be laying there, stuck in this weird, sunless city with you, wondering where Zwinny is?!"

"Look, just calm down. A lot more time is passing than you think. You were hit hard. It's been hours since Joel assaulted you." I growled with frustration, standing to my feet and pulling at my hair.

"Yes! I was following him!" I roared. "What was he doing there?! Zwinny said he was investigating! What's going on at that motel?"

"Nate, I've already gotten upset and tried to find a way out. It's no use. You just have to wait. The good thing is, time moves really fast here. Try not to get worked up."

"That's really easy for you to say," I argued. "You can see anything you want!"

"I can't leave," she pointed out. "At least you'll be gone soon."

"How do you know?" I asked, impatiently.

"Look, just sit down. I'll tell you what I know," she reasoned. I was breathing heavily, looking at her. I swallowed, taking my seat next to her.

"My name's Dee," she spoke. "Um, my half-sister, B, is basically the reason your mind, or whatever it is, is here right now with me. The motel you're unconscious in is this business venture that B set up around the time she met Thom. Do you know Thom?"

"Yes," I answered. "I met him today."

"Technically, you met him yesterday" Dee argued.

"Whatever," I said. "Keep going."

"B started this whole thing in order to help people, I guess. The way I see it, what she started, she can't even undo, and she doesn't completely realize the extent of what's going on. The motel feeds people these "safe doses" of danger. B believes it's an environment that is completely under control. Thom did too, but now he's started to realize that things are slipping through his fingers. Now, John … John hasn't slept."

"Probably cause he killed a dude," I said.

"He hasn't slept since he got to the motel a few months ago," Dee continued. "The funny thing is, he's so tired—sleeping little bits every now and then—that sometimes I see flashes of him here, leaning up against a lamp post or stretched out on a bench in really quick, random moments."

"How can your sister assume that anything she's doing is safe?" I asked. "I was at the motel for less than an hour, and I witnessed all the worst parts of a post-apocalyptic Vegas. How can Thom and John ignore what's happening?"

"I don't know," she replied. "I'd like to say it's because of how much they think they're helping people—namely the girls."

"Well, Kristy sure seemed appreciative," I said.

"It's weird," Dee agreed. "They all are."

"Do you know anything about Zwinny?" I asked her.

"Well, as each of you guys have been added into the equation, the situation has only gotten worse—"

"I haven't done anything," I interrupted.

"It's science, man. The mere fact that you guys are a part of this thing in some way, shape or form is collateral damage. I know it's not directly instigated by you personally, but you added to it by bringing Zwinny and her dude into this. Hell, I even added to it. I died. Thom found some strippers. Feel better?"

"I don't know what any of that means …" I said.

"Look," Dee started, "everybody's got a part to play in disarming it. I think mine is probably talking to you. When Thom came along, the Moss Head Motel thing turned into the monster that B couldn't handle. The oil kept coming, so the monster kept growing. Thom didn't start the damn thing—he just managed it because B couldn't. John got thrown in right when B was needing to expand. Then stuff just started getting even weirder. B picked up all these new girls, and then John notices his ex-wife, Kristy, is one of them."

"John is Kristy's ex-husband…. That makes sense," I noted.

"Yeah, so the reach is so big that it's coming full-circle. Last but not least, there's you. You've still got this freakish, sick thing with Zwinny, so you try to pop her fiancé for something stupid in some weird attempt win her back."

"Why were you so easy on Thom and John?" I asked impatiently. She ignored me.

"So in the process, Joel gets killed and Zwinny's

fiancé, a dude just trying to do his job, gets shanked, and now he's bleeding all over the place."

"Someone's got to tell Zwinny ..." I said with a sudden change of heart.

"Oh, so you're not seven anymore?" Dee asked me.

"I'm sorry! I've been in a heartbroken, love-drunken rage. I know I need to clean all this up. I just wish I could get up ..."

"Wow," Dee said. "I'd hate to think that the key to getting over someone is getting your ex's new interest stabbed in the neck, but damned if that wasn't exactly what just happened to you."

"I'm not over her, I just realize that none of this is worth it," I protested.

"I just wish I could have conversations with all of you like this. If I could speak to B and the four of you like this, you might all want to go back and fix your messes."

"Three of us," I corrected her.

"Oh. Forgot. There's another one," she added casually. "He's been trying to cover it up instead of clean it up, but he's just making it worse. You're going to have to get a hold of this kid if you want to help Zwinny." I could feel myself becoming frustrated again.

"How do you suggest I find this person and help Zwinny find her fiancé if I don't even know when or if I'll ever wake up?!"

"Ah, you'll wake up, you little bitch," she said. "Calm down. You're day here is probably almost over. As soon as the sun goes down, you'll wake up back in that room.

"There is no sun," I observed. "How can you tell how long a day lasts here?"

"Weird! You don't see it?" Dee asked as we both looked up. "At least there are still mysteries in heaven or in your brain or in the glow-in-the-dark metropolitan nightmare zone or wherever we are. Hopefully the mysteries will last. I used to get so freaked out by the concept of eternity. I could think so deep about it that it would cause me to almost go into cardiac arrest. Now it doesn't. I still don't get it, but it doesn't trip me out anymore. There are some things the human mind just can't comprehend. That's how you know there's bigger shit than you," she concluded.

"I think that was the most sage-like thing you've said this entire time. I always imagined that people in dream worlds would talk to me like those omniscient god characters from video game cutscenes."

"Not much longer now, brave warrior," she joked. Suddenly, I began to notice that the light and colors around me were fading quickly. Since the last time I looked, the buildings had all but disappeared. The world around me was shrinking faster than I could take note of. Every place I looked suddenly vanished before my eyes. The swing set had now gone. The grass was blackness beneath my feet once again. It was happening so fast. All that remained was Dee's figure and the chain link fence, the color of which was now fleeing the dark, becoming smaller and smaller as it raced towards us at an alarming rate. I followed the speed of it right up to Dee's hands. They were disappearing. I looked into her eyes. She knew what was happening.

"How will I find him? What's his name?" I asked in a panic. But she was gone.

Again, I stood in utter darkness. I knelt down to feel the ground. It had become asphalt once more. I was reverting to my previous state, traveling back to my body at the motel. I suddenly remembered the color of Dee's green eyes, and then my eyes began to feel sticky and wet. I could sense that I was almost awake. The pain in my head pulsed, almost causing me to feel sick to my stomach. That's when I became fully awake. It was then that I noticed my body was covered in sweat. With my middle and index fingers, and keeping my eyes closed, I slowly reached to my left, knowing that Joel lay beside me. I felt his waist—stiff with death—and quickly recoiled, wiping my face with my sleeve. Once I had rolled away from him, I slowly opened my eyes, rubbing them to alleviate the unbelievable pain bolting through them to the rest of my skull. I gently touched the top of my head. It was a mixture of dry and wet textures. The pillow felt the same way, and there was some sort of diaper of bandages that had fallen off my head.

I tried my best to breathe only through my mouth. I know it had only been a night, but I didn't want to take the chance of smelling a dead body. I had enough trouble with expired milk. The room was dark, but light was peeking in through the curtains. Though my body felt too weak to move, I willed myself to stand out of the bed. I got up and made my way to the door. I opened it slowly, letting light into the room and allowing my eyes to adjust as it revealed Joel's body. It wasn't as bad as I thought. His face was sunk in a bit, and his skin had begun to turn. He lay there with yellow teeth fully exposed, his long hair matted to the pillow.

I slowly peeked my head around the door. The sun was still incredibly bright, but it no longer hurt my eyes. I saw several women walking here and there down in the parking lot, but none of them saw me. As I made

my way down the stairs, I noticed that my feet felt
swollen and hurt to walk on. I reached into my pocket
and pulled out my phone in hopes that I could get a
hold of Zwinny, but it was dead. My guess was that I'd
been lying up there for maybe twelve hours. I stumbled
my way into the office where I had met Thom yesterday
or whatever. The door was wide open, and a
screensaver of weird shapes and colors now danced
wildly on the computer monitor behind the desk. The
office was empty as I had expected. I had to see what
time it was. I slowly moved behind the desk and
abruptly shook the mouse to make the dancing images
go away. Minesweeper was still on the screen. It hadn't
been touched. 10:15 A.M. on February 14th, 2036.
Perfect. I was sixty now. Ok, so my guess was close.
About twelve hours.

As hard as it was to believe that I had been lying on
my back, conversing myself through another realm all
night, it actually wasn't as weird as some dreams I'd had.
While standing there behind the counter, I quickly
found myself scouring the room for food. I was
starving. There was a quarter machine in the
corner—you know—one that has three different types
of candy that could be ten years old, but you'd never
know. There were Runts, Red Hots and Reese's Pieces.
I searched aimlessly through my pockets and the
surfaces around me for quarters or any kind of change
but couldn't find anything. I cranked the knobs
fruitlessly, then turning my attention to Thom's pot of
coffee. I felt the glass vessel, half-full of room
temperature black water. I grabbed a Styrofoam cup,
poured myself some and dumped several ounces of
cream and sugar into the liquid without measuring,
stirring vigorously with three or four straws. I tossed

the sticks on the floor and slammed the drink, retching as I finished. The additives had hardly dissolved, leaving the sensation of bitter rainwater chased with sugary sludge.

I wiped my mouth clean and glanced through the open blinds of the window and noticed John climbing into the camper on the far side of the lot. I decided I'd stop by on my way to see what was left of my car. As I traveled across the blinding, white parking lot, I noticed several girls and other patrons of the motel getting ready for the night's activities. As I approached the trailer, I could hear voices coming from the inside. I walked up and knocked three times, backing off the steps with one foot. The door opened, and John stood there, looking just as he should have—curious and at a loss for words. A woman inside, whose figure I could barely see, shouted from behind him with urgency.

"Don't just let him stand there! Bring him inside, goober!" John stepped aside, holding the door open for me as I crawled in. Those first few seconds were incredibly awkward. Thom stood in the kitchen, a young blonde girl (not Kristy) sat on the couch next to who I assumed to be B, and John stood behind me, closing the door. They all politely stared at me.

"Hello," I said. "Can anyone tell me why I spent the night with a dead guy instead of in a hospital?" They looked at each other, apparently not ready for my forwardness. They remained silent. "OH, believe me, I've got more questions than just those," I said. No one moved, then the woman on the couch spoke,

"Of course you do. First, I need to apologize for these tards that work for me. They wanted to send you off with the detective, but I told them I wanted to speak with you as soon as you woke up. I was going to have a doctor friend come over and hook you up to one of those Gameboys or whatever they are that do the 'beep—beep' thing. When I called him, he said you may or may not come back, but here you are! I'm B, by the way. This is Bobbie. That's John and that's Thom," she said, gesturing here and there. She was wearing a red shorty robe with pink hearts on it. I'd almost forgotten it was Valentines Day. Bobbie wore some shorts and a child's t-shirt.

"Yeah, we met. Where's Kristy?" I asked. John seemed to bow up.

"Why?" he responded.

"Just wanted to see if she was alright."

"She's fine," he said. Dee had mentioned that Kristy was John's ex, but I couldn't tell if anyone else in the room knew.

"I need to find the guy who got stabbed. You said he was a detective?" I asked. Thom finally spoke up.

"Not happening, man. We can't risk that. He's under someone else's supervision."

"Is he going to die?" I asked.

"… Who knows," Thom replied lazily.

"We're not bad people," B interjected. "We just can't afford to have these kinds of complications on our clock."

"This guy," I said, pointing to John, "shot someone to death!"

"In self-defense—" John interjected and then stopped suddenly. Shock filled the room. The four of them looked at each other with eyes wide.

"How did you know that?" Thom asked, looking at me.

"I saw it happen!" I yelled, suddenly remembering I'd been knocked unconscious before John even showed up to the situation. The room was silent for a moment.

"He's gotta go," B said to Thom and John as they seized me by the arms.

"Wait!" I yelled. "Aren't you worried I'll report you to the police?! I'll report this whole place! I'll flip you upside down! Tell me where he is!" I lashed about wildly, shoving and hitting each of my captors numerous times until I felt cold gunmetal against my cheek. John was pointing his weapon into my face.

"Baby, come on …" Bobbie reasoned with him. B stood up and walked towards me. The guys were holding me still. I couldn't move. B and I stood almost face-to-face.

"We don't know for sure what that guy was up to. No one's come looking for him; probably because no one cares. It's been twelve hours. Honestly, you're probably the only person who even knew he was here; you and the other off-duty cops who saw him but wouldn't say a word. So as soon as the he's dead or better or whatever, we're in the clear."

"Yeah, well he's not one of your dirty beach cops," I argued. "What about my bed buddy in 201?" I replied. "What do you plan on doing with him?" The expressions in the camper were vacant. No one knew how to answer the question. They had no idea what they were going to do with the body. "You're serious … you're just going to let him rot up there and stink up the entire beach …"

"We're working on it," Thom said, nudging me to the door.

"You guys can't possibly think there isn't a clean soul in this town who will question what happens out here every night," I noted. "This whole thing just got a lot bigger."

"You're right, and you're not helping the situation," Thom said as he and John grabbed my arms and escorted me out of the camper. "Let's take a ride."

"Where?" I asked. "Are you taking me where they took him?" Thom and John looked at each other. "So, let's see—murder, prostitution and kidnapping! You guys are racking up!" Thom and John dragged me from the camper. "Kristy!" I yelled, half hoping to get her attention from somewhere, but she didn't appear. I was taken to a green Jeep and then cuffed and had a pillowcase put over my head. They laid me face down in the backseat and took my wallet and cell phone. Thom made a quick phone call and then they got in the car. I resisted the whole time, but it didn't matter.

For the next twenty minutes, I rolled around in the back compartment of that car like a two-liter in a grocery bag. I tried my best to discern where we were headed by following a mental map based on the turns and stops we had made, but I lost track several minutes in. When we finally stopped, Thom and John exited the car without me. After several minutes, I was drawn from the car and guided maybe twenty yards down the dirt road. The smell in the air was something obvious, but for the life of me, I couldn't figure out what it was. The darkness from the blindfold and the hard, gritty surface beneath my feet reminded me of the place where I met Dee. Softly, in the distance, I could hear footsteps slowly coming up the road toward us as we continued to walk.

Though it was difficult to make out, I thought I could distinguish at least two people walking—maybe three. The steps came closer and closer. I could tell whoever was moving me had noticeably quieted. No words or greetings were spoken, as I'm sure the two groups came within normal speaking range of each other. We were almost upon them. Our pace slowed as the sounds from our feet blended with theirs, and our shoulders brushed past each other's. My sense of smell was heightened from being in the singular presence of death for so long. I immediately smelled sweat and sour clothes mixed with a sweet scent of some earthy perfume. As our groups passed through each other, I had to know.

"Who's there? This is Nate Flemm——!" I said quickly as a hand covered my mouth. But it was too late. She had heard me.

"Nate!" It was a voice I recognized very well, but nothing followed but muffled screams.

Book IV

EZRA

My name is Ezra Cotton. I live on a farm that boards horses for people too rich to ride them or too poor to pay us. I have three older brothers; all with names from the Bible just like mine. Their names are Job, Saul and Nehemiah. They like to screw around a lot and get mixed up in shit that I don't have the time or patience for. They stopped trying to recruit me ages ago. Realized I wasn't giving in. Had more important things on my mind. By the time I was ten years old, I'd sold my first horse (even though it wasn't mine to sell) to a man down the road. My brothers were so busy sticking their fingers in their butts that it took them a week to realize I had all this money. Took my parents even longer. The short version is, I had my brothers working for me that summer, pawning our whole farm away. I got raped for that one.

My parents both have names from the Bible, too. I've never read an inch of the book in my life, but Ma told me they were—right after I asked her what the hell kind of name Ezra was. Ma's the kind of woman you see on the Lifetime Channel—a tragic, tiresome woman with a wardrobe as fixed as a cartoon character's. Moses Cotton was a meaty, less intoxicated version of Pap Finn—only we were too old to beat. He would never admit it, but I'm sure he was at least a little bit frightened of us by now. I know the rule. No son can whoop his dad, but we'd get damn close. We called him Moses because he always told us that a man's use can only be measured at the end of his life by the number of times his name was called. I hadn't ever planned on being a dad, so it didn't really matter that much to me.

There was a basic rule that if you were around when work needed to be done, you did it. No questions asked. My brothers seemed to be pretty content with the idea of lazily hanging by the barn, doing chores and dicking around whenever they had time to spare. Their wages were food on the table and a roof over their heads; although, we were aware that a decent breeze could blow the roof right off of our doublewide. Naturally, me getting a job at Airlux, an industrial air conditioning manufacturer, instead of working for Moses on the farm for free, quickly alienated me from the rest of my family. Ma would say, "you aint doin' nothin' to help your daddy and his brothers! You just run off and make your own money and forget about your family." Moses wouldn't say anything. The Cotton men just showed indifference towards a person they were in disagreement with. I could care less. I was making money, and I had no intentions of staying around that farm forever, playing grab-ass with my brothers.

It didn't mean I always escaped the daily jobs of a farm; in fact, Moses and my brothers would take any opportunity they could to get me outside during the day—stripping stalls, letting horses in and out, driving oats from one side of the property to the other on our golf cart/horse food delivery conversion vehicle. Most of the time, I slept long and hard during the day and worked the graveyard shift at Airlux. Let's put it this way, if I woke up on the farm during the day, it was a mistake. Evenings were usually reserved for my girlfriend, June. That's another thing they loved. If I was with June at the house, they'd find any and every reason they could to get me doing something pointless. I suppose the easiest thing they could do to distract me was get me to go smoke with them. We were all regular smokers. Even Ma took a drag every now and then, but

114

smoking is definitely something you do in a corporate setting. It's a social thing. That's the only reason anyone does it. It's the same principal as when girls travel in flocks to the bathroom. Women pee together. Men smoke together.

June would come back there with us and smoke her own on the terrace sometimes. Actually, I guess it really wasn't so much a terrace as it was just a sort of big deck that looked out over the pasture. Anyway, June earned a lot of unspoken respect from my brothers because she smoked. Then she lost every ounce of that respect because of her tattoos. Apparently, my brothers have no problem with a woman smoking, so long as she doesn't have unsightly ink across her neck or shoulders. Moses hated it the most. He'd never said a word to June. Said all kinds of things about her when she wasn't around, but he didn't care for tattoos, either. Ironic thing is; Ma's got a tattoo on her ass that Moses didn't even know about. It's of Jackie Robinson. What does that say about their relationship? I don't know.

We were circled up out there one day, sitting in the old patio furniture, fanning dogs away like flies, kicking them and such when Job piped up excitedly,

"Neil, you hear what happened to me and Saul yesterday?" Neil was our childhood friend who'd spent about as much time on the farm as we had.

"Nah, what?" He'd ask. We all took drags of our cigarettes. Me, June and Saul liked Marlboro Lights. Job and Moses smoked Reds (though Moses only smoked alone), and Nehemiah smoked Camels. Neil didn't smoke.

"So, me and Saul were down around the old stalls trying to find something to knock this beehive off the back of the barn with. Saul notices a metal canister—like an old aluminum keg or something with a mole cricket painted on the side and a hose coming off it with a nozzle attached. He grabs the thing and I mean, it's slap full of something."

"I'm getting bored," Nehemiah groaned.

"No, no. Listen," Job continued, "here's the best part. The canister is air compressed, so we give the thing a few good pumps and take it over to the rat hole to try it out."

"Rat hole?" Neil asked, puzzled.

"You know, the gap in between the shavings and the tack room," Saul replied.

"Oh!" Neil said.

"Yeah, there's always rats in the there," Saul concluded.

"So anyway," Job continued, "I take the can and spray into the hole to see if we can flush a couple out. The second I do, one big ass rat comes hobbling by, falls over and dies right there. So, we're like, dang, this is some powerful stuff!"

"Then I took the can, cause I wanted to try it out on something a little bigger," Saul interjected. "So, I took it over to Nelson's cage, you know, Gina's pig?"

"Yeah," Neil replied, laughing.

"Well, Nelson still won't go anywhere near Saul," Job said, "because he still hasn't forgotten him trying to feed him that pork chop." They all laughed.

"That's animal cannibalism!" June yelled. "No wonder!"

"Pigs can't tell what they're eating," I said to June, "and pigs don't hold grudges," I told Job. The four of them were burning new cigarettes.

"Listen!" Job urged. "So, I take the end and stick it right in his nose."

"I can't listen to this," June protested.

"I only used a squirt of it. Nelson starts losing his shit—stumbling this way and that, licking himself, squealing like crazy—and then he falls asleep. Right there!"

"That's hilarious! Let's go do it again!" Neil insisted.

"We can't! He's still asleep! He's been asleep for like twenty hours straight," Saul laughed. June wasn't too thrilled. I didn't really care. She was used to it enough by now that I wasn't worried about her.

"Well, let's do it to a horse or something," Neil suggested. Neil was always wanting to take things just a little too far. He'd broken countless things on the farm out of his dire hunger for destruction. At least, that's what we all argued. They truth was, hurricanes and other weather had irreversibly changed our farm, but we still liked to joke that even the tin roof on the barn was caving in because of something Neil did up there.

"Well, I haven't finished the story yet," Job smiled. "Saul was all about giving a dose to that runt that Beckins hasn't paid for in months—"

"Moses would be happy if that thing died," Nehemiah said.

"Well," Job continued, "Right then, Beckins actually shows up!" Job and Saul laughed.

"As we're standing there ready to poison his damn horse!" Saul added, laughing. Neil and Nehemiah smiled, eager for more details. June was ignoring the story, playing with one or twelve of the dogs. I'd forgotten how many there were. I continued to smoke and listen as the sun sank below the trees and the cool air began to set in.

"Saul starts immediately spraying around the edges of the barn door, like he's the Orkin man. Beckins comes up to me, says he needs to speak with Moses. I tell him he's out getting panels, but I'll take a message. He brings me over to his truck, says he's got a Godload of axle grease. Says he's made an arrangement for the last two month's boarding costs. I asked him what the hell Moses would need six barrels of axle grease for, and he says Moses needed it for something he's mending."

"That old yellow piece of shit tractor covered in shrubs out back?" Neil asked.

"I don't think so," Job answered. "I have a feeling it has something to do with what's in the cellar of the old barn. Moses has been mending something down there since before any of us were even here. Back when he was just a worker. Before this was even his land."

"Cellar?!" Neil exclaimed.

"Shut up," Job whispered quickly. Everyone quieted down as Moses came through the side gate. We sat there, silent and contemplative, taking drags off our cigarettes as he walked up the steps with his wreathy beard, meat belly and saggy boots. His skin was dry as a baseball glove and about the same color. He had been slow-baked by the sun for almost sixty years. When I heard the term "redneck", I'd often think of that scaly, wrinkled expanse of leather that wrapped around behind Moses' ears, but it was never funny. He may have never gone to college, but he had seen more of long days than any of us ever would. None of us made eye contact. We tried to appear as if life were too toilsome to converse.

Once Moses had gone inside and closed the door, Job continued in a cautious whisper.

"There's a cellar door out beside the old barn," he explained.

"Why have you guys been keeping this a secret?" Neil asked, aggravated.

"It's no secret," Saul answered. "It's just that no one's allowed near it. Job tried to get in there when we were younger. Moses has some kind of mental security system around that place. If so much as a piece of hay is bent in the wrong direction, he knows. Not to mention, Moses told us to never go near the place. Job got destroyed for that one."

"Did you get to see what was inside?" Neil questioned.

"No. Not even close," Job answered. "He got me before I touched the handle. Pinned me to the wall of the barn, man-slapped me and dragged me back to the house."

"Geez! How old were you?" Neil asked.

"Eight," Job replied, "But, anyway! back to the story at-hand! Alright … Did I tell you about the grease?—Oh yeah, never mind. Ok, I remember. So, Saul wanders out to the front of the barn where me and Beckins are talking, and then I just proceed to mess with him!" Job and Saul started laughing again. "I say, 'Beckins, you realize you're almost four months behind in fees?' and he says, 'yeah, that's why I'm bringing your daddy all this damn grease!' and I go, 'look, I appreciate the gesture, but it's going to take a hell of a lot more grease than this to both ease your debt and get our work done.'"

"Since when are we selling tractors?" Nehemiah asked.

"We're not. I lied," Job said leaning in, ashing his cigarette and sharing looks with me and Saul. "So, Saul

119

starts to lose it. I can hear him holding back laughing over there by the fence, still spraying that God-awful poison on ants or whatever. It's taking everything in me to keep a straight face with Beckins. So, he says, 'I made an agreement with Moses. Four barrels of grease. Four months of pay.'

"So, knowing what a push-over little prick Beckins is, I put my hand on his shoulder and look him dead in the eye," Job said, grabbing onto Neil's shoulder theatrically with a his cigarette hanging from his mouth, "and I said, 'Lucas, you may have made an agreement with Moses, but you didn't make an agreement with me.' Then I proceeded to make up some crap about laws and what-not. I said, 'county statutes say that if a horse, livestock or head of cattle remains under another man's care, unpaid for more than four months time, it becomes his property.'" Nehemiah and Saul laughed hysterically. "And you know how much he loves that damn horse. So, I say, 'I want sixteen more barrels of this stuff by the end of this week, or that sorry excuse for a horse is mine, and Saul over there,' I said, 'if it were his, he'd kill it right now.'" The boys laughed again. Even I smiled at the thought of poor ole' Lucas Beckins' face.

"What's going to happen when Moses sees him unloading sixteen more barrels?" I asked. Something I said caused Job and Saul to laugh even more. I looked at June. She was walking back up to the house from far off.

"That's the best part!" Saul laughed. "Damned if he doesn't love that dirty old horse, cause he was back before the end of the day! We had them unloaded and into the old silo before Moses ever got back with the panels!" The back deck was a circus when June came walking back up the steps and sat on my lap. Neil piped up again.

"I just don't know how you guys can ignore what's going on down in that cellar."

"It's bolted up with a lock and chain, man. It's no hope. Forget it," Saul concluded.

"So, what are you going to do with all of it?" I asked.

"We don't know yet. We'll figure something out," Job replied, taking a final drag and standing with the rest of the guys to go inside.

June and I stayed. She looked at me and put her arms around my neck. I sat there, pushing her hair behind her ears, forming my fingers into a circle and letting them fall the length of her light brown ponytail that diminished and escaped my hand halfway down her back. She smiled.

"I'm so glad you're not a douche like your brothers and Neil."

"Thanks," I said. "Even though I'm the youngest, I've always felt like I was their older brother, always dropping whatever I was doing to bail them out of some sort of trouble."

"It's really only Job and Saul who are the problem. Neil and Nehemiah just tag along with everything. They're like dogs," she said, looking at our herd of K-9s. "All it takes is one of them to set the others off, and it only takes one for the rest to lose interest. If Job and Saul would just chill out, I think your brothers would be pretty normal."

"You're so wise," I joked. I kissed her. I had been with June Johnson for just over a year now, and that feeling had never gotten old.

That night, I was working in coil braze at Airlux. It was a world controlled by robots, and we humans just supervised them while they made our basic necessities. This is how it went—there were these huge mechanical arms called "manipulators" that lifted enormous rolls of aluminum and fed them into stamping machines. These machines then cut or "stamped" the aluminum sheets into the smaller pieces that were stacked into metal baklava, which we call "fens"—the stuff on your outdoor air units at home that you scratch your name into with sticks as a kid. These fens house the actual copper hairpin coils that the Freon travels through. When the fan blades suck the air through the fens and past the copper hairpins, voila! Air conditioning.

This guy named R.J. was our Unit Supervisor. He'd come around at least once a night to piss us off as best he knew how. He never really rode anyone else that much, but he sure had it out for me from day one, and I have no idea why. Maybe it was my farmer's work ethic. Maybe it was my quiet way and subordinate behavior. Whatever it was, R.J. was never slow to tell me what a shitty job I was doing.

"Did your mom teach you how to braze, son?" he'd say.

"Nope. No sir, she didn't." I'd go on with the job, hoping to ignore him away, but he'd just snatch the torch out of my hand and shove me to the side. I'd bite my lip to near bleeding—thinking about the power of MAPP gas and how easy it would be to accidentally Luke Skywalker that prick's arm clean off or feed him to the cogs.

"I swear. You guys are dumber than a hooker!" he'd say. R.J. was known for spending lots of time soliciting prostitutes from an underground ring that used a strip club as it' cover. One day, I'd expose him and get his ass fired. "… Idiots …" he'd mumble under his breath as he walked away.

"I hate this place so hard," Stan would say. Stan was the guy who worked in the cells beside me.

"This is going to be a long night if Douche Canoe keeps dropping by. We've only been here two hours. Feels like a damn witch's eon," I replied. A "witch's eon" was a made up unit of time or travel that a Southern workman uses to describe a long time. We were standing there, brazing all manner of connections that came down the line. Unlike welding, brazing used MAPP gas instead of electric. Silos filled with the gas, fed pipes throughout the plant. Those pipes were then dispersed into smaller pressurized hoses attached all over to handheld diaphragms where two nozzles split off and bowed back towards each other. One side shot out the MAPP gas. One side shot out the oxygen. When the two components combined at the striker (a small box that produces a spark), the result was a blowtorch with a super hot flame that could melt lengths of Zinc Aluminum alloy bars onto the connections of the coil, preventing leaks. I liked knowing how the stuff around me worked. At least that way I felt a little more connected, but it didn't help on a night like this. I was getting aggravated.

Now, I'm not without my own mischief. I wasn't afraid to make things happen, even if the way that they happened was a little less than upstanding. I've been known to cheat at poker, steal an occasional beverage from the gas station or strangle a neighbor's dog if it was barking too much. Right now seemed to be one of those times—calling me to liberate myself, or at least give myself the night off. It was 2 A.M. and I wasn't into it. Today had been one of the days where I woke up too early and had Moses and my brothers on my balls about unloading a flatbed full of galvanized steel gate panels, so I was tired. Airlux was huge on being alert and awake while on the assembly line for safety purposes, so that's how I justified what I was about to do. Plus, R.J. was just pissing me off more than usual tonight.

"Stan, you have a quarter?" I asked impatiently. Stan pushed his safety glasses up, discharged his torch and reached into his pocket.

"Vending machine's broken. Just forewarning you," he said, giving me the coin.

"Ah, I don't care about that. Give me your gum, too." Stan gave me a weird look.

"Come on, quick. It's for your own good." He spit out his gum and put it in my hand, questioning me with his expression. He laid his gas down and watched me curiously as I rolled the gum in my hands to dry it out and stuck it to the back of the quarter. I walked over to where the manipulators were lifting the aluminum rolls and feeding them into the stamping machine. When no one was looking, I stuck the quarter to the sheet of metal and walked to the water fountains. I looked over at Stan. Upon seeing what I did, he quickly went back to brazing, pretending not to notice. Within seconds, the aluminum was being loaded into the cutter. Before I even made it back to my cell, this terrible sound of grinding gears and colliding metals came crashing across the plant. The guts of the stamping machine were immediately burnt up, and the entire plant erupted in cheers and applause. I had successfully procured a night off.

Before it was 2:30, Airlux had clocked out and emptied into the parking lot. Not much that can be done with a burnt up fen stamper. Hopefully the cameras didn't catch anything. I always figured they were fake anyway. I knew Stan wouldn't rat on me. He couldn't stop talking about how brilliant it was.

"That was amazing! But you know R.J.'s going to be looking for a reason to pin it on you when they finally get engineers in there."

"I don't care. There's no way he can prove it was me. It's not like the time Collins threw his dad's pocketknife in there. That thing was like a family heirloom that he'd shown everyone in the plant. Guy was an idiot. He might as well have thrown his driver's license in."

"What if they finger print it?" I stopped dead in the middle of the parking lot, giving Stan the "are you serious?" face. We kept walking.

I got home around 3:00 and noticed that the barn light was on. It had to be the Cotton brothers up to something. It sure wasn't Moses. He was an energy Nazi. Every once in a while, you'd see him walking around in the barn at night with a flashlight because he didn't feel like using the power. I parked and made my way up the red clay path to the barn. You could tell our barn from a mile off. Above the doors, neatly hewn into the weathered planks, was an enormous cross cutout—a relic left by the barn's previous owners. On a dark night, the lights from the inside escaped through the hole and painted the likeness of a great sword made of gold whose blade pointed straight and true at the colossal structure. From the air, I imagine it must have looked like some medieval omen, shedding its light on some unfortunate Camelot.

As I entered the barn, I heard voices coming from Moses' "office," the brothers' usual late night sludge spot. Upon my opening the door, Job, Saul, Nehemiah and Neil burst into laughter.

"We were just saying how uptight you'd get if you walked in right now and found out what we did tonight!" Job laughed.

"Wait till you find out what I did tonight," I smiled.

"Wait, us first," Saul said. Everyone quieted down. "Shut the door," he said, as Neil closed it behind me. "We just brought BP early!" Saul said excitedly.

"What do you mean?" I asked, confused. Job continued.

"Remember those sixteen extra barrels of grease we told you Beckins brought us? Well, me and Neil popped one open this afternoon and started slinging it all over each other. Stuff's like a thick, black goop that you can almost ball up in your hands. Well, we showed Saul, and he automatically had a crazy idea." The boys laughed some more. Saul chimed in.

"We loaded up six or so barrels onto Moses' big four-horse trailer and went out to the old pier close to Banger Grill, where Neil used to work, and we unloaded!"

"You've got to be kidding me ..." I said. "How much?"

"Well, just one," Nehemiah said. "We didn't realize how far it would go."

"We did like a hundred yard section," Neil said.

"And then called it in," Job laughed. I was shocked.

"I'm sure you guys are aware of this already, but you know you will go to jail if anyone finds out about this ..." I warned.

"Well, we'll never hit the same place twice," Saul explained.

"What?!" I interjected. "You're going again?!"

"Hell yeah, we're going again! This is our masterpiece!" Job added.

"When?" I asked.

"I don't know. We'll give it a few days," Job replied. Don't get me wrong. It seemed like a phenomenal prank, but the brothers had gone in too deep this time. "You guys are idiots," I said, opening the door and making my way to the house. Job peeked his head out the door.

"Don't tell anyone, Ezra."

"Believe me, I won't," I replied, lighting a cigarette.

"Hey! You never told us what it was you did tonight!" Job said, as the other guys emerged from the room for their smoke break between laughs.

"Don't worry about it," I answered, maneuvering around the sword.

One week passed. Every morning, I'd come back and check the trailer to see if the Cotton brothers had used more of the grease. Twice, they had. They were using it sparingly—only one barrel every few days. It was no shock when the local news began featuring updates on the "spills" that I assumed to be the work of my brothers. The locations were pretty systematic. That's what made me suspect it had to be. Anytime I'd ask them about it, they'd just laugh and smoke, laugh and smoke—until one morning when things seemed to change. I came home at around 8 A.M. and noticed Nehemiah and Job smoking wildly and making loud gestures near the fallen oak tree adjacent to the barn. Though I couldn't hear them, I could tell they were yelling at each other. I got out of my car and slowly walked towards the house, never once taking my eyes off them. I'd almost made it all the way to the front stairs when I ran into something rock solid.

"Whadya reckon they're pissin' over?" boomed Moses. I turned abruptly, stumbling back and picking up my keys. He was smoking with one hand and had the other stuffed under the opposite arm, leaning against the rail.

"Eh," I cleared my throat. "... it's probably n-nothing," I replied. Moses looked at me suspiciously, silent at first.

"Mmm," he grunted. He was psychic. I took one last look at Job and Nehemiah and headed inside before Moses asked me anything else. I already knew too much. I stayed awake, sitting up on the back deck smoking to make sure I wouldn't miss them when they came out to burn a couple.

Before I'd lit my second cigarette, Job, Nehemiah and Saul came trailing through the back door, each taking their usual seats and kicking their usual dogs. They didn't seem to be themselves at all, quietly lighting up and rubbing their foreheads in stressful silence.

"Someone saw you guys, didn't they?" I asked. All three of them looked up at me and then at each other. Just then, Neil came rolling out the door, already retrieving what I thought was a cigarette but turned out to be a wad of twenty dollar bills.

"Here's my part. Everyone else paid up?" He asked, slapping the money on the glass table. Saul looked at me followed by everyone else. Nehemiah slapped Neil on the back of the head. I knew it was only a matter of time before they told me anyway, so I just asked.

"What happened?" They hesitated at first, but soon, Saul began to spill.

"Last night, after we finished up, we went to No Hands to have a couple drinks. We were all a little toasted, but this moron right here," he said, motioning to Job, "pays for a lap dance with this hot blonde, and ten minutes later, we're getting pulled into the back by this big bald dude. Apparently, Job here got a little too comfortable with Bobbie Big Boots and started letting the details fly about our recent project."

"You are such an idiot ..." I said to Job. He was still shielding his eyes with his hand.

"Don't worry, we've been telling him all night," Saul continued. "Anyway, baldy calls the owner in—this MILF in a smoking jacket, like she's Hugh Hefner. Her name is B. She sits down in front of us and informs us that she heard, through the grapevine, about the grease." Saul took a deep breath, glancing at Neil and Nehemiah. "One thing leads to another, and before you know it, she's threatening to report us unless ..."

"Unless what?" I pressed. Nehemiah spoke up.

"... Unless we keep her paid up," he said.

"What? Who is this chick?!" I asked, baffled.

"Look." Job finally said, standing to his feet. "I screwed up, but we just caught a break, and that's all that matters!"

"How much does she want?" I asked. The guys hesitated, looking back and forth between each other. They were so reluctant to tell me anything. "Come on! How much?"

"... She wants ... Fifty thousand ... over the next year," Job said. I was the one burying my head in my hands now. "If you think about it," Job continued, "it's really not that big of a deal. If you do the math, it's like a thousand dollars a month for each of us."

"No, actually," I said, "it's a huge deal for you guys. I bet you don't make two thousand a month between the four of you. If you do, you don't keep it."

"You saying you want to contribute?" Job asked sarcastically.

"No. Hell no. Of course that's not what I'm saying," I replied.

"You're right, though," agreed Neil. "We don't make enough to pay her off, especially if you guys don't pull your part! At least I brought what we agreed on."

"Well, everybody better take initiative and figure out their own way to get two fifty a week on this table, or we're going to jail," Saul said, patting Job on the back as he, Nehemiah and Neil stood up and went inside.

Job and I stayed on the deck, sitting quiet as ever. I stayed because I hadn't quite finished my second cigarette. He stayed because he was going to ask me for help.

"So, listen," he started. I took a long drag and breathed out. "Look, I wouldn't ask you if it weren't for …"

"Weren't for what?" I asked.

"… We think Gina might be pregnant." My eyes closed halfway and I put out my cigarette.

"I'm not even going to continue to tell you what an idiot you are. I'm sure you already know that, and it seems like you're aware of the fact that a daddy in jail is no good."

"You're the only one of us with a real job. You make more than one of our whole payments every month. You don't want us to all go to jail do you?" Job asked.

"No!" I laughed. "That's why I told you guys to quit all that while you were ahead. I warned you something like this would happen! 'Oh! We're going to hit different places every night!'" I said mockingly.

"Fine," he said, getting up to go inside. "I just thought, since you've got yourself sort of a business mind, you might know of a way to help us out."

"Too bad you can't work it off," I said. Job stopped.

"That's a great idea!" Job said excitedly. "I'm pretty sure the guys would be up for anything, honestly." We sat in silence for a minute before Job started again. I could tell what was coming. "I just wish we had somebody to negotiate this thing for us …" I got up to walk inside, pulling out my phone to call June before I went to sleep. "If you didn't get the hint, I'm talking about you!" Job added. I looked at him, annoyed.

"… I'll get back to you when I wake up …" I said. Job stood aside as I opened the door and went in the house.

When I laid down to sleep, I had a dream about Moses. It was late at night. I was in the house, and all the lights were off except for one moving about in front of the kitchen window. It was a small orange dot that looked like a firefly or something. As I watched it hover around, I realized that it was actually coming from outside. I went to the window and looked out. The firefly was actually the ember at the tip of Moses' cigarette. He was striding out across the pasture towards the old barn. Though everything was dark inside the house, I could see that the moon was full and the sword was brightly stamped along the grass just outside. I went out into the night air and followed Moses, being sure to keep my distance.

As he rounded the back corner of the loft, I watched him approach the cellar. He bent down, lifting a flat stone beside the cellar door and producing a small key. I watched silently from shadows of the old yellow tractor. He loosened the lock and chain, lifted the door and then, as if he knew I was there all along, he looked straight at me. At first, I was frightened. I moved back.

but then I realized he wasn't angry. He kept eye-contact with me as he stamped out his cigarette on the cellar door and threw the lock and chain over his shoulder, disappearing below and leaving the entrance wide open as if to invite me in. I moved immediately and eagerly approached the gaping, black rectangle in the earth.

I looked back at the house to make sure no one was watching me, and then I began my descent. The darkness didn't last long—only a few steps. I was looking for Moses' cigarette firefly, but it wasn't there. I could hear pieces of metal clanking together, and I began to see the shapes of short people or kids forming to one side. Once my eyes adjusted to the scene before me, I saw Moses standing there with my three brothers situated on their knees in a straight line. He had taken the chain from the door and bound Job, Saul and Nehemiah to three posts near the wall of the cellar which now looked to be a simple four wall structure with a black barrel in the corner and various support beams anchored in the dirt floor.

Their faces were of stark fear. I was afraid that Moses would lock me up with them, but I could soon tell that wasn't his intention. He walked over to the barrel, preyed the lid open and stuck his hand in. It was the thick, black grease that the brothers had been messing with. Moses took a handful of the sludge and walked over to Job, forcing his lips apart and shoving the grease into his mouth. Job refused, and the brothers and I protested, but Moses was too strong. He repeated the process with Saul and Nehemiah, each one receiving the goop more forcefully than the last. Finally, the attention turned to me. Moses and my brothers were staring at me. Their mouths were stained black.

That was the last thing I remember.

Several hours later, I woke up wondering what the hell it could have possibly meant, but it didn't matter. I had made my decision. I went out back for a smoke and found all four culprits talking over the prospect of me helping them out. I didn't even say anything, I just went to my usual spot, kicked a dog out of my chair and lit up, rubbing my forehead between drags.

"Look, Ezra," Saul started, "I know Job is the oldest, but you've always actually been the responsible one." This was weird talk for Saul. It almost felt nice. I didn't like it, so I discouraged it.

"Whatever. I think the line between us is a little more specific than that. It's more like, you guys are dumb-asses and I'm not," I said.

"Dang. Left my phone on the toilet," Nehemiah said, getting up to run inside.

"Get me some tea," I demanded, glancing up at him. He stopped and stared at me. Everyone on the deck exchanged looks like, "what the hell did he just say?" but no one said a thing. A minute later, Nehemiah was handing me a big glass of Ma's syrup. This would have been like moving mountains before. Everyone, not just me, suddenly noticed a shift in respect at that table. I took a sip.

"You guys better hope I'm able to arrange something that doesn't involve money," I said, putting my feet on the table and taking a drag, "or you guys are going to jail." There was an excited stir on the deck. Job smiled.

"Do you need a ride over there?" he immediately asked, ecstatic about my decision.

"No. I think I'm going to just go over there alone," I replied. Everyone at the table shifted and sat up, like they were going to protest my decision. Saul spoke first.

"Ezra, don't you think it's best if at least one of us goes too? I mean we don't want to seem like weak-asses—shoving our little brother in to fight for us. It might piss her off."

"That's exactly what it's going to seem like if you go with me. I want it to feel like I'm coming in there as your attorney or something, with an alternate plan that she has no choice in. If you guys want me to do anything about it, it has to be like this," I said. They looked at each other without exchanging any words, and then Job looked up at me.

"We owe you big for this, man."

"Yeah. You do. I'll be thinking of what that'll be," I replied.

Ten minutes later, I was on my way over to a strip club in the middle of the day. I wasn't really sure what I'd be able to do for my brothers and Neil, but I knew that what they should be more afraid of—more than going to jail—was Moses Cotton. He wouldn't be upset from a disciplinary standpoint—he'd be pissed that he'd lost his entire workforce. They'd be beaten half to death or shot before the police ever came screaming up our driveway to haul them off. I didn't want the family business to go under, but I had a feeling all of our professions were about to change.

Pulling into the parking lot at No Hands Fran's was like pulling into the courthouse at 7 A.M. for jury duty. It was honestly the last place I wanted to be, but I needed to go in there like I knew exactly how it was going to turn out. I slid through the double doors of the club a little less confident than I'd hoped and walked up to the bald butcher at the bar.

"I need to see her," I said confidently. He looked at me for a minute then turned around and picked up a portable phone, punching a couple buttons with his fat fingers.

"Got someone up here says he needs to talk to you," he mumbled into the phone. "Ok. Bye." He clicked it off and set it down. "She'll be out in a minute. You can have a seat," he said, gesturing to the closest mirror-top table. I looked at it but didn't walk over immediately. "Or you can stand right there. I don't give a shit," he grunted as he threw a towel over his shoulder and walked into the back. I could hear the radio playing somewhere. They were giving the latest local oil report and sounding quite optimistic because there hadn't been any showing up within the last few days. It was funny being one of the only people in the world that knew why.

Before I even had enough time to take in my surroundings, a tall, full-bodied woman emerged from the back wearing the same clothes that Saul had described. She was looking around—right past me—as if I wasn't even there.

"Are you B?" I asked. She looked down at me, surprised.

"Oh! Hello, fella," she said. "Who's asking?" I extended my hand.

"My name's Ezra. I think you met my brothers last night?" She shook my hand and looked up, trying to remember.

"Oh! Right! You're not coming to fess up, too, are you?" She laughed.

"No. I'm coming to rearrange your agreement," I replied. She laughed again.

"You're coming to rearrange my agreement with your brothers. Ok," she smiled. Clearly trying to entertain me. "Let's hear it. What do you suggest?"

135

"Do you mind if we sit?" I asked.

"Oh, please. By all means!" she playfully insisted, pulling a chair for me.

"Well, I'm hoping we can arrange a work exchange or something," I said, taking my seat and pretending not to notice that she was making fun of me.

"Are you and your brothers interested in having sex for money?" She asked.

"… Are you being serious?" I replied.

"Well, I don't need any work done around here. I feel like my business is growing outward more than inward, but no, I'm not being serious."

"I heard the same," I said.

"Oh?" she replied.

"Yeah," I started. "There's a guy I work for who's paid every single one of your girls for sex at least twice." I could tell she was starting to get frustrated.

"You know, prostitution takes two," she said. "That's what's beautiful about this business. Makes the dude look real slimy. Locks him into an automatic non-disclosure agreement."

"Well, he's not afraid to disclose," I said.

"So what are saying?" she asked. "You going to rat me out unless I agree to change terms with your brothers? Do you understand what I do here?"

"You own a strip club that's a front for a prostitution ring," I answered.

"Wrong!" she snapped. "Geez, I'm going to have to start printing little pamphlets with mission statements on them for people like you. We're saving lives here. Any one of these girls could leave any time they want, but they stay because here, they're protected and valued. You really want to try to ruin that?"

"If you're such a saint, then why would you be trying to blackmail my brothers for a stupid prank?" I insisted.

"The tall one," she started. "Job was his name I think? He got a little belligerent with one of my girls when she wouldn't let him touch her. He started losing it and talking about how he owns this town and does all this crazy shit all the time."

"So why didn't you just kick him out?" I asked.

"Well, he had already blabbed everything to Bobbie before I got a chance to send Bledsoe over," she explained. "I thought, why bother? We'll handle this ourselves."

"Wait, you mean Sheriff Bledsoe?" I asked.

"Yeah. He gets in for free. I see him myself. See what I mean?" she smiled. "What else you got?"

"Look, I think that if we talk through this a little bit, you'll find that we can come to an agreement that helps you out a lot more than money will."

"What's better than money?" she asked.

"Business. Exposure. You said yourself you're wanting to grow outward," I reminded her.

"So, you're saying, somehow, you can get me more clients outside the club?"

"Yes. That's exactly right!" I explained. "Like, I know for a fact that my boss has bragged openly about banging one of your girls somewhere on the beach once."

"Yeah. The beach has been killing this week because of BP and all the clean up. Those oil guys are horny as hell." B paused and looked down for a second. "Look, I'm sorry, but your brothers are out of luck."

"They'll never be able to pay you the fifty thousand," I said.

"Then they're going to jail, I'm afraid," B interjected, standing to her feet and turning her back to me.

"So, you'd rather be out of money and out of help too?" I asked. She started to walk away. "Look," I said. "I know a few seconds ago, you realized the exact same thing I did." B stopped, still facing away. "My brothers are the only reason you've had such a profitable week on the beach. What if they could keep that momentum going?" I couldn't believe what I was suggesting. B turned to face me.

"You think I haven't already thought about this? In an economy that is failing because of oil, I'm preparing to explode as soon as it shows its face out there. And soon enough, it will happen naturally," she said.

"But," I interjected, "you know as good as I do that it's been weeks since the spill, and their saying we may not ever see any of it here. That is, unless we bring it ourselves." B paused, biting a nail and tapping her slipper on the floor.

"If this works, it could be huge for us," she said, pausing again briefly. "… Alright, but I don't want them losing their minds out there. I don't know where you got the fake oil, but you better make it last, and you are going to be in charge of them," she ordered. I started to protest, but immediately realized it would be the best way to guarantee that nothing stupid happened again. "I want you to be my correspondent," she said. "Tell me how things are going."

"Ok. So we have a deal … no more money, just oil?" I asked.

"Yes. And can you get them here tonight at like 11:30 so we can decide how we're going to go about this?" she asked. Suddenly I remembered I had a job. I could call in sick easily enough tonight. I'd have to figure out something more long term if I planned on making this work, but this came first.

"Um, ok. Yeah, I can do that," I said.

"Cool," B replied. "That guy sounds like a total douche canoe, by the way. Is he?"

"Who?" I asked.

"The guy you work for who blabs about my girls." I laughed a bit.

"Yes. Yes he is," I said. "Later."

On my way home, June called. I'd totally forgotten about her today. She was upset that I'd used my entire afternoon to stick my neck out for my brothers. She wasn't really jealous that she hadn't gotten to hang out with me; she was just more concerned about how I spent my time and energy—fixing other people's problems.

"Ezra, I just care about you! I don't want you to get mixed up in crap your brothers get into just to save their asses like you've done your entire life," she said.

"I know. I really think it's going to be ok, though. I think I'm going to have to try and switch to another shift," I explained.

"You see? This is what I'm talking about! Because you feel the need to clean up your brothers' messes, our relationship now has to suffer. I work in the mornings, Ezra. If you can't get an early shift, we'll never see each other." She had a point.

"Look, I'm sure I'll be able to get on mornings, but this is necessary, June. Think about what could happen if we don't do this. Our farm will go under, and my family will be in huge trouble. Do you really want my brothers to go to jail?" I asked.

"No, of course not. I love your brothers, even though they can be real idiots sometimes," June said.

The truth was, she may have been really upset, but my brothers were going to love me. They were going to worship me. Things had eternally changed in the Cotton house.

"This is awesome!" Saul yelled. "We're off the money hook, and we still get to slather grease on the beach?!" The brothers cheered and congratulated each other, thanking me most.

"Man, we can't ever repay you for this. How'd you do it?" Job asked.

"Well, first of all, just because you guys are of the hook with the money doesn't make this a risk-free venture. There is still the very real possibility that we will get caught."

"We?" Nehemiah asked.

"Yes," I said. "We. And you guys are now my bitches. What I say goes. There isn't going to be any arguing or anyone challenging my authority. I am now involved and that means you listen to me. B instated me, herself."

"That's cool, man," Job said. "You are the king."

"Yeah, you say that now, but when we're out there and one of you thinks you've come up with a brilliant idea, and you stop listening to me, there will be failsafes in place," I explained.

"Failsafes?" Neil repeated.

"Yeah," I answered. "B's not an idiot. She won't be overrun. If she put me in charge, that's the way it's going to stay."

That night, the five of us went out to the horse trailer and silo to take inventory and see what we had left and how we could best make it last as long as possible. We then crammed into my car to go have this meeting with B. I guess we hadn't taken into consideration that the club would be slam full of people. Job, Saul, Nehemiah and Neil all looked pretty comfortable in the place. I'd never been to a club before this afternoon. I wasn't even much for hanging out in bars. I tried my best not to look at the dancers. For some reason, I was worried someone would think I was dirty, but who was I kidding? The brothers led the way to a table that they apparently always sat at. Before long, B came walking out from behind the stage. From what they told me, B danced at least once a week. They must have come here more than they let on.

"Hello, boys," she yelled. My brothers and Neil didn't say a thing. They just nodded and smiled. The pulsing music was so loud that it pretty much discouraged talking altogether.

"How's it going?" I smiled.

"Let's lay some ground rules," B said, producing a map of what looked like the beach west of Indian River. "This is where you guys first dumped your oil?" she asked, pointing.

"It's grease actually," Neil yelled. We all looked at him.

"Yeah," Saul ignored. "Right here near the end of the Walk, at the old pier."

"Ok. This is The Moss Head Motel. It's where I'm camping out," B yelled. "I'd say you guys should probably hit this entire stretch, heading as far west as you can until you hit condos or some sort of civilization, then probably start back in this direction. Once, maybe twice a week. Mix it up a little bit. I don't care. The motel is really the last decent establishment for the cleanup to gather at for the next forty or fifty miles, so I'm not worried about our patrons going anywhere."

Nick May

"What happens when we run out?" I asked.

"Don't … or figure out how to get your hands on more … grease," she looked at Neil. "I really don't want to see you guys after tonight. Just convince me it's real. That's all I want. Ezra here is in charge. I know he's your brother, but if he so much as makes a peep that any of you are ignoring what he says, I'm sending Sam over for a talk," she said, gesturing in the opposite direction. We all turned to observe the enormous barman fist pumping with one arm and pouring a glass of scotch with the other. We slowly turned back as B continued. "We're going to make this last as long as possible. Everyone cool?" We all nodded and agreed. "Ok. Good. Ezra will get your numbers for me. Take the map. Take notes. Try to improve. It's called good work."

"Yes, ma'am," Job yelled obnoxiously during a pause in the trance music. B stared.

"Cute," she remarked. Everyone looked at Job and then humbly agreed with B. "Oh, one more thing," she said, closing her eyes. "Please don't get caught …" She stood up.

"Not a problem. Thanks a lot," Saul said.

"Yeah, thanks," Nehemiah agreed. We all smiled at B. She was powerful in our minds.

"It's best if you probably never come back in here either," she said. With that, we scraped our chairs loudly backwards like high school kids leaving lunch and made our way to the door. "Ezra!" I heard B call. I turned. She was leaning on the bar. "Can I talk to you for a second?" she yelled, motioning me over with her finger. I walked back over.

"Come out to the motel tomorrow night if you want. It's marked on the map. I'll be in the camper. I'll show

142

you all my 'dirty stuff'," she said.

"I'm sorry?" I choked.

"You know. I want you to be on our side about things. I know we started a little on the rough side but just come see what we're about.

"Oh. Ok. Sounds good. I'll see you then." I turned around and headed back out. Tomorrow would be vital for me. I'd need to get some things in order, including changing my schedule to mornings in a last ditch effort to save my relationship. I knew that over the course of the next few months, I wasn't going to be able to devote much time to June. This made me feel sick inside—putting her on the back-burner—but that's where I was.

On our way home, during the wee hours of the morning, we decided that our first official strike would be tomorrow night as soon as I got done at the motel. I have to admit, besides the fact that we were now the slaves of a female prostitution tycoon; there was something a little bit thrilling about the planning of elaborate hoaxes. You're a lot more thorough with sneaky plans when it could mean the difference between being free and being in jail. It doesn't mean I wasn't still abnormally stressed and intensely annoyed by my idiot brothers.

Before we'd even gotten back to the farm, everyone had been assigned specific duties. Job's would simply be just to get us a regular supply of grease from Lucas Beckins. That's it. Saul would engineer the entire operation. He'd figure out little things like the most efficient way to sling grease in a timely fashion or what's the most authentic-looking type of coverage? How can we get rid of little things like footprints? He was also first in command when I wasn't around. Neil and

Nehemiah would hold the map. They'd keep track of where we'd been, and they'd scope out areas and report on their findings. They were also our containment control which meant that they, by any means necessary, were to prevent others from witnessing our actions. My job was to micromanage the entire thing and get us out of this crap as soon as possible.

I invited June over in the afternoon. At least we could hang out while I tried my hardest to switch shifts at Airlux. She was sitting there next to me as I nervously called the number and tried my best to get a hold of that prick, R.J. I waited for twenty minutes and spoke to three different people before they finally got the guy on the phone. I knew this was going to be hard.

"You've got R.J." he said.

"Hey, man. It's Ezra."

"Who?!"

"Ezra Cotton. I work in coil braze."

"Oh, did someone already tell you?" he asked.

"Tell me what?"

"You're fired. Hope the night off was worth it." He hung up. I put the phone down, wearing a blank face that June could see straight through.

"What's wrong?" she asked. I breathed.

"Ok. Look. The other night, I did something kind of stupid," I said.

"Did they just fire you?!" she interjected. I pressed my lips tight together.

"The other night, I broke one of the machines on purpose so we could go home early."

"You what?!" she yelled.

"Somehow, they found out it was me," I said. "Couldn't be Stan," I mumbled under my breath. June was rubbing her forehead in frustration.

"Ezra. That's something one of your brothers would do. You're a sweet, smart person. Why would you do something so stupid at the cost of losing a good job?" she asked.

"Hey," I snapped, "I'm not a goody goody! Sometimes, people piss me off and I do unpredictable things. That's what you signed up for when you started dating a Cotton ..."

"Well, you'll certainly have lots of spare time to spend with me now," she said.

"Listen, June, I love you, but I am seconds away from not only losing my job, but my mind, too. Somehow, through some brotherly obligation, I've tied myself into an agreement that could last for God-only-knows-how-long in an attempt to prevent my entire family from going under! By extension, this involves you, so I'm going to need some cooperation and support from you. You may not understand, but you have to help me by having the best attitude you possibly can." June came and sat on my lap like she always did.

"Ezra ... I'm sorry. I know you don't want to be in this anymore than I want you to be. I want to help you. Just tell me what I can do,"

"Maybe we should just let things sit for a while," I said. June's face started to change. She never cried—just got really stoic. I continued, "I can't expect you to understand the obligation I feel towards my brothers. Just know that no matter what happens, I love you and I want to be with you when it's all over."

"Ezra, what are you saying? You want to break up right now when you just said you could use my support the most?" June asked. I reached for both of her shoulders.

"It's wrong for me to ignore the fact that I'm about to be way in over my head with some really messed up shit, and I have no right to pretend that I'll have the time to devote to you. Plus, I don't want you connected to these people."

"No, Ezra," She said firmly. "I'm sorry for complaining and giving you a hard time, but there's no reason for that. We'll make time to see each other. It's not like you're going to war."

"I know, I know. Look, the way I see it, she can't own us forever. Eventually, the whole reason we signed on in the first place will become more and more irrelevant. We're only getting her business rolling for her. Soon, she'll be out of our hair,"

"Whatever. I promise I won't be a bitch. You have my word," June said.

I loved her attitude about everything. That was her best quality. She just wanted to help—even if it meant there would be a strain on our relationship for a while.

I immediately felt better about things and more able to focus on the situation in front of me. The pressure was off. That was the most important part for me. She was being extremely cool about it when she had every right to be pissed. As far as losing my job at Airlux, I could really care less. I felt I was becoming more like my brothers anyway. Why not relapse into farm work as well? I was honestly relieved to be out of there. Sticking that quarter to the man was one the best decisions I had ever made.

That night, I was trying to slip away from the house unnoticed so I could head to the beach and let B show me whatever she wanted to show me. It was harder than I thought—getting away without anyone really seeing. When I was eating dinner, I noticed that I was being watched really close. As if I didn't feel like my family was keeping tabs on me already, it seemed as if everyone was watching me to see what I would do next. Ma' Cotton was oblivious. She was the least of my worries. It was actually Moses who was starting to show real signs of suspicion. I slipped away from the family at a moment when I knew Moses was occupying the back deck. Knowing that I had to get past him somehow just seemed a little easier than getting past my three brothers and Neil. Just as I reached for the doorknob, Ma' saw me.

"Headin' to work early?" She asked, still unloading the dishwasher. I turned.

"Nah, I'm not working there anymore," I replied.

"I see. Going to get some tattoos with your girlfriend?"

"See you later, Ma'," I said, opening the door.

"Seems like that's all I ever hear from you anymore. 'See you later, Ma'.' It's that kind of thing that causes families to fall apart ..." She muttered. It was hard for me to not just lay into her right there and explain all that I'd been doing to prevent this family from losing any good name it had left. No one on Earth could make me as mad as Ma'. Her assumptions caused more fights than I care to mention.

As I stepped outside and shut the door, I noticed Moses standing on the opposite side, near the grill, completely covered in darkness. All I could see besides his black shape was the small orange glow of his ember and the smoke rising in the moonlight. I didn't say a word—just headed straight for the steps.

"You quit or get fired?" Moses asked in a low boom. I stopped in the grass.

"I broke a machine. They fired me," I replied.

"You never were good with equipment." He took a drag. "That's why I never let you near my tractor," he said. I stood there quietly for a second—trying to think of a way to move the focus away from the tractor which was further from the topic of axle grease, but Moses was a shark. "Speaking of …" he began. I bit the inside of my lip. "Any reason Beckins would leave me a message about buying one of my tractors?" Why would he be asking me that?

"… Maybe he's got some work to do …" I said hesitantly.

"I don't got but one tractor …" he interjected. I slowly turned to his silhouette, still producing smoke in the corner. The ember's glow was opening and closing like a cat's quiet eyes. I tried my best to seem oblivious.

"… Hmm …" I replied. He waited. Then, Moses said something I'll never forget.

"Well … I'll tell you one thing: if I find out you boys are trying to make me look like a dumbass in front of my customers … I'll kill every last one of you." The ember brightened intensely. I didn't say a word. I just stood there for a second to prove my respect (the way they tell you to behave if you encounter a moose in the wild) "You seen my flashlight?" Moses asked out of the side of his mouth.

"Which one?" I replied.

"Any of them …" he said.

"No. Haven't seen any," I answered, walking off casually towards the gate. I knew he wouldn't ask me where I was headed. He didn't care.

I guess the first thing that gave the motel away was the set of tour buses at the front. Then I saw the Winnebago. There were a few people scattered here and there, but for the most part, it seemed dead—like the

148

motel hadn't seen business all winter. I pulled up to the old travel trailer that had definitely seen better days. I got out and knocked firmly on the door. I entirely expected a humble servant to answer, but instead, it was B, herself.

"Come on in, sweetie," she said, with a motherly purr. As I stepped inside, I noticed the stale smell of popcorn and ass. "You can pop a squat on the couch right there. There's a pen and paper there if you wouldn't mind writing the names and numbers of all fourteen hundred of your brothers.I'm just going to finish up these dishes." I sat on the couch, pulling out my phone to find their numbers. "So, I just wanted to clue you in on exactly what's going to be happening here over the next however many months."

"Alright," I said.

"Basically, the oil cleanup, or 'Hazwopers', as they're apparently called, arrived this past week with the help of your brothers. They'll be parking here at the motel, waiting for calls, and riding the buses out to the spill sites. Some of them have already begun finding modes of entertainment for themselves. Well, we're about to bust the place wide open. I've just made an arrangement with the owner. We'll pay him a fee for allowing us to have free reign here."

"I have a question," I interjected.

"Sure." B said.

"How much oil cleaning crew could possibly come? You'll cap out soon," I said.

"The Wopers are just a spark," she said. "Dirty people draw dirty people. Haven't you ever been to Walmart in the middle of the night?"

"Yeah," I laughed.

"Same principle," she said. "So, we'll really ham up the spills around here. Get the officials really scared so they'll send more Wopers. The rest is snowball. As soon as people hear what's going on, they'll come in by the droves—as well as other 'vendors' I'm sure—which is why we've already purchased all the rooms. We'll rent them out as more stuff comes."

"Vendors?" I asked.

"Right. Yeah, like ... other things that people are interested in. People who like prostitutes. What are they into? Get it?"

"Yes," I replied. "So what happens when police show up?" B smiled and widened her eyes at me, holding the coffee pot in her hand.

"We invite them in!" she said, immediately going back to the glass pot. She was staring intently at the dark brown ring around the inside. "I can't get this damn stain out!" she growled.

"I'm not going to keep asking seriously about cops. I'm sure you've got it under control," I said, continuing with the names and numbers.

"We've got it under control," B absent-mindedly repeated, now squirting Windex straight into the coffee pot. "Oh. Ez ..." she said. Ez. Like Ezra was too long.

"Yeah," I answered.

"This is the other thing: In order to maintain a level of anonymity here, as far as who's behind what, most of our big name girls will remain in town at Fran's, and we'll just be recruiting for here as we go and using unknowns from the club as well. I'm going to try to check in at Fran's as much as possible, but I'll probably end up out here full-time if things get big. I'll be out of sight, of course—here in the ole' Windbag, but I've just recently hired a guy who will be overseeing things for me. He'll basically be an extension of me—a me that people don't see. After tonight, you'll report to him. He'll report to me. In fact, it's probably best if you're never seen here at the motel. You guys can work that out."

"Are you going to introduce me?" I asked.

"Oh. His name is Thom," she replied. "T-H-O-M. I know. It's weird. I'll give him your number. You'll probably never see him."

"Ok," I said, handing her the completed paper. B leaned on the counter—her cleavage clearly visible—looking at me with her head resting in her hands.

"So, how are you guys doing with everything," she asked as she turned around to reach high for something in a cabinet. The bottom of her butt cheeks peeked at me from beneath her shorty. Maybe she was younger than I thought.

"Uh, well, weeeee aaaaarrrrr …" I began, clearly distracted. She reached higher. I snapped out of it and looked away. "We've got enough grease to last for a while. We're working on getting more. We figure we'll hit in sort of a once-a-week, twice-a-week sequence. We'll stagger it, you know?"

There was a rumble outside. A door slammed shut and the trailer shook. Just then, the door to the camper swung open, and a burly looking dude with long hair came stomping up inside and shut the door. I didn't say a word. I just looked at B who had stopped scrubbing the coffee pot and had grown an angry face.

"Joel, what are you doing here? Who even told you I was here?" She asked, annoyed.

"Where is he?" he asked, looking at me briefly.

"He's not here," B said. He looked at me.

"Who are you?" he asked, as if my presence offended him.

"Someone who's about to beat your ass if you don't get out of my face ..." I said calmly. I was by far, the smallest Cotton, but that didn't have anything to do with my curiosity. I had a high pain tolerance, so I usually just liked to test people. Most of the time it worked out.

"What did you just say?" he asked, stepping towards me. My less cautious side took over. Before I could even think, I got up from the couch and choke-slammed him against door. The whole camper shook. B quickly braced some plates in the cabinets that were about to fall. I got right in his face.

"Get out," I said. He swung for my head, but I caught his fist in my left hand and twisted his arm back down towards the door handle and threw the lever. He fell backwards out of the camper and landed with his arm behind him, bending backwards and shooting bone straight out of his backwards elbow. He screamed like there was no tomorrow—lying there on his back in the white gravel with blood pouring from his arm. I looked back. B was standing by the sink, with both hands covering her mouth and nose.

"Please tell me this is not a problem," I said, holding the door open. Joel was screaming loudly. B let her hands down, smiling slightly.

"... I really wish I could keep you in my pocket," she said.

"Ah, you'd be better off with one of my brothers," I replied, turning towards Joel.

"My business isn't with you, you piece of shit! I'll find him, B!" he yelled, rolling on his side with tears and spit bubbling from his dirty face.

"You actually might want to find a hospital first so a doctor can sew your arm back on," I replied. He screamed again. I shut the door and sat back down on the couch. "Who is he?" I asked. B walked over to the window and looked through the blinds.

"He's leaving." She came and sat down beside me. "That's Joel. He's my ex-boyfriend. He's also my baby daddy."

"Don't say that," I added quickly.

"What?" B questioned.

"'Baby daddy'. Don't say that. It's grammatically incorrect and really dumb."

"He won't let me see him," she went on, ignoring my comment. "I sent Thom over there the other day, so now he thinks I've got a new boyfriend. He's looking for Thom."

"So, the guy is trying to control your son and your sex life?" I asked.

"I know. He's crazy. I haven't even slept with Thom yet," she replied. "Well, you've gotten your first taste of what it's like to work for me. Still thinking it looks better than jail?"

"Yes," I replied. "Are we done, or do you need anything else?"

"No. I think we're good. It was nice to meet you, Ezra," she smiled. "See you never."

"You, too," I replied.

Later that night, I met up with the brothers and Neil down at the parking lot at the old pier. They had crammed into Job's truck and laid the barrel of grease in-between two spare tires in the bed. Apparently this is how they'd been doing it so far. We all lit up and stood in a circle at the back of the truck.

"How's it look?" I asked Job.

"Well, we've got about half in this one," he said, extending a hand over the side of the tailgate. I saw Beckins early this morning and mentioned that we were starting a tractor sales and maintenance business and would need more grease. I said maybe we could work out a deal. He seemed really happy about that. Said he needed a new tractor and wanted to be our first paying customer," Job laughed.

"Yeah. That's probably why he left Moses a message this afternoon asking about buying one of our tractors," I replied.

"Shit," Job said.

"Yeah. Clean that up," I said. Job nodded. "Ok, Saul, how are we going to do this?" I asked.

"Ok, well, the last few times, we sort of developed a way rolling it between our palms, with sand" Saul said. "Then, you just pitch it into the shallow water and the tide kind of washes it up in a real natural pattern. I compared it to stuff I saw on the news in places like Orange Beach and Pensacola. It looks pretty dead-on. It also eliminates the footprint problem, too. We just all stand in one place. Should only take us six or seven minutes with all five of us."

"Alright, whatever. Ok. Neil, Nehemiah … where are we going?" I asked, standing on my toes to see out over the truck. Nehemiah took a drag and pointed west.

"We've basically already hit everything from where the Walk ends all the way to Access 31 or 32—"

"So we were thinking of like starting a little further up at the fort tonight," Neil interjected. "It's super dark down there and if we can get up on the wall, we'll have good cover in case anyone comes."

"Alright," I replied. "Are we all riding together or separate?"

"No, no, no," Neil warned. "We can't just go driving up in there. The road's closed since the hurricane, anyway." Nehemiah hopped up into the truck bed and removed one of the tires holding the massive barrel in place. As Saul lowered the tailgate, Nehemiah pushed the barrel with his foot, rolling it off the edge of the truck and sending it slamming to the asphalt. The noise was unbelievably loud. Hushed cursing whispered across the parking lot. Everyone took a whack at his head when he got down.

"Don't be a cousin ..." I said. "... Someone hand me a flashlight." No one budged. "Are you serious? I told someone to grab flashlights."

"We couldn't find any—" Neil said.

"Moses loses them all," Nehemiah added.

"Well, I guess we'll just have to let our eyes adjust ..." I said sarcastically, shutting the tailgate and marching them off into the black sounds of the Gulf.

Every few nights, we'd meet somewhere, go over the plan, and roll the barrel off towards the sizzling waves. The first couple weeks were mildly entertaining—the entire effect of slinging tar and then driving past the motel to watch how it all would change and grow. A lot of times, the road along the Beachside Walk was bumper-to-bumper with people trying to get to the motel. On weekends, the Walk would usually be full of people going here and there, back and forth, but eventually, the flow started to move all in one direction.

After a while, it started to feel like we were hosts of a huge party that we weren't ever allowed to go to. I hadn't heard from Thom once, so we just kept doing our thing for weeks. We weren't even getting close to running out of grease, so we hadn't even considered Lucas Beckins again. Moses seemed to be as clueless as ever. He and Ma' were usually in bed and long-gone before we ever even left the farm. We found ourselves driving further and further, only to turn around and repeat the process in the opposite direction. The job was easy—just tedious. We were never spotted. We were hardly ever even within sight of another soul for miles and miles in every direction. Occasionally, we'd get a close call, but nothing serious.

It was all happening so very fast. I got to see June more than I thought I would. Had I not been so occupied, it would have been a whole hell of a lot harder on my thoughts. The worst part of that was the guilt I experienced after going an entire day without thinking about her once. She'd call me, send me a text or just show up in my room and interrupt my sleep to be with me. I was such a dick. But then I thought about the alternative. I didn't want to see my brothers go at this alone and possibly end up in jail. Regardless of how pissed the whole thing made me, and how much I wanted to strangle each one of them, loyalty was a disease in my family. We had to accept what fate had handed to us and become brothers again for the time being. The night was our new dominion, and we'd forgotten all about who we were before the oil.

———

We'd spent two months slinging grease, and we'd covered the entire beach more than twice over before we finally got a call from Thom one night. I didn't know what to expect, but when I picked up the phone, he ended up sounding pretty friendly.

"Hey, Ezra?" he asked.

"Yeah ..." I answered.

"Hey, man. This is Thom. I work for B. I don't know if she told you I'd be calling."

"Yeah. Been waiting for two months," I said.

"Ha!" he laughed. "Well, we've gotten a little busy over here. We've got more people than we really understand how to manage. Needless to say, whatever you guys are doing out there has worked."

"Well, that's good. Can we stop?" I asked.

"Actually, that's what I was calling about. Where are you guys?"

"We're out here about a mile or two west of the fort, about halfway done."

"Oh! Great! Do you think you guys can come by?" he asked.

"Um … sure," I hesitated. "But B said she didn't want us at the motel ever …"

"Oh, no one will see you. We can meet in the alley out back."

"Ok. Should we go ahead and finish this one?" I asked.

"No, no. Don't worry about it. Just head on over. Bring everybody," he said.

Within minutes, we were packed up and gone—leaving a half-finished oil job on the beach. It was still worthy of a cleanup, but nothing special. The back of The Moss Head Motel was like the back of a Spencer's or something. As if you don't already feel dirty enough just walking in the front of a hippy store like that. As we pulled around, we noticed a younger-looking guy sitting in the open at a small table of some sort with a candle lit at the center. There were cars coming and going. A guy was getting out of one that was full of hookers from the looks of them. He stumbled out, holding a gas can as they drove off down a dark road out of the back of the motel.

The stranger at the table (who I assumed to be

Thom) got up and greeted us as we poured out of the truck and walked over.

"How's it going guys?" he shook our hands. "Come on over here and have a seat," he said, pointing to several boxes, crates and a stump all gathered around the upturned wooden cable spool table. We sat down. I took the stump.

"Sorry for calling you guys over on such short notice. Also, I'm sorry for not calling you sooner. It has literally been insane here the last couple months," Thom said.

"So you can tell a difference since we started?" I asked.

"Oh, absolutely! We're probably now bordering on fifteen hundred to two thousand people per night. I mean, they can't all get in here at once, obviously, but that's like the numbers that a big night club would run, I'm sure."

"Wow, man," I said.

"Yeah, you guys have definitely exceeded what we had originally hoped for. So, on that note, we need you guys to stop." We looked at each other, and then back to Thom. "At least for now. It's just becoming too much to contain. I tell B this and she doesn't believe me, but there's really only so much you can do in a town this size. I mean, she's got plans to move to these old condos down the coast, but I don't think that will ever happen. Anyway, I'm getting away from the point. We can't afford to continue growing right now, so what we'd like to do is keep you guys around to do some ghost jobs if you want."

"What the hell is a ghost job?" Saul asked.

"Yeah, well, I like to think of you guys as like colonial minutemen, right?" Thom suggested. "Basically, whenever we have a situation or a need, you guys will jump in at a moments notice and clean it up. No one will ever see you. It's just another level of secrecy that keeps things ambiguous. I used to be able to do things like this, but even now, I'm becoming way too much of a public figure."

"What kind of situations are you talking about exactly?" I asked Thom.

"You know, like, say we find out someone is cheating at the tables, John and I bring them to you guys. You guys make sure he never shows up again. Simple as that," Thom said. "Also, we may end up needing the occasional oil spill or diversion. Who knows? The point is, B's not interested in your debt anymore. It's not realistic. She gets that, but she just sees you guys as very handy and wants to pay you to have you stay on and just do whatever we need." Neil and the brothers all looked hopeful. I, however, was looking forward to calling it quits and getting back to June. "You guys take some time to talk it over. I'll be back in a little bit," Thom said, getting up.

"Alright. Thanks," I said. I waited for Thom to clear the side of the building and then turned around. "I don't know, guys. If we've finished what we started, shouldn't we just get out while we can?" I reasoned. "There's no telling what we could end up doing."

"Wait, Ezra," Saul said. "You're the one who's always saying you'd rather work for a stranger than for Moses. You just got fired."

"I know, man," I agreed. "I know I'm not the one who should be turning down work right now, but I can't help but feel like it's just going to bury us deeper."

"Come on, man. At the very most, we're bouncers …" Job added.

159

"You heard what he said," I interjected. "We'd be a secret. They need people in this type of position so if we get caught doing something, they can just cut us off and pretend they never knew!"

"I don't know, man," Nehemiah said. "It sounds like a pretty good deal to me. Basically we just get to sit around until something goes wrong or they need us to sling more grease."

"Yeah, but what happens when something actually does go wrong, and you guys really do get thrown in jail and can't do anything about it?" I asked.

We sat there and argued for the next thirty minutes until we finally heard something like muffled gunshots in the distance. This was not the kind of place I wanted to be employed. It certainly wasn't the kind of place that my delinquent brothers needed to be employed. I was trying to make that very clear. Just then, Thom came walking quickly around the corner. We could tell he was in a hurry. He was breathing heavily ... and holding a gun. We stood up.

"You guys decide yet? Because I've got your first paycheck if you want it," Thom said.

"Thom ... what just happened?" I asked. "Were those gunshots?"

"Yes. You are correct. Those were gunshots, and your first job has come early. I've got five hundred for each of you. You guys in or out?" He asked, looking at everyone but me.

"I'm in."

"I'm in."

"I'm in."

"I'm in," came the resounding answer from everyone but me. I stood there as they stared at me, waiting for a unanimous vote. A glimpse of June shot through my head.

"Whatever," I caved. "Let's just hurry. What happened?" Thom crouched down.

"Alright. Everyone sit. This is the deal. In a couple minutes, a few friends of mine and a guy named John are going to come out the back door down there by the office," he said, pointing across the alley. "They're going to have a guy with them who's really hurt. He's been stabbed. He's bleeding all over the place. I want you guys to handle it."

"What, like take him to the hospital?" Saul asked.

"Absolutely not," Thom replied sternly. "Just handle it."

Suddenly, the door on the far end of the building swung open and shed a pillar of light into the dark alley. Several guys were assisting the stab victim out the back door of the office. He was moaning. The rest of the guys were grunting and straining out words the way a group of overweight movers would while trying to lug a washing machine up a set of apartment stairs. "One more thing," Thom said. "He's a cop." Good to know. We immediately jumped to our feet and ran for the truck, prepping our makeshift ambulance for the ride to wherever we were going. Someone threw us a couple blankets that we laid in the bed of the truck. Within seconds, the guy was sandwiched in between the tires and the grease barrel and Neil and Nehemiah were situated on the wheel wells at either side of him. I looked at Thom.

"So, you say no hospital, so where should we take him then?" I asked impatiently. Thom stopped what he was doing and looked at me firmly.

"… Handle it," he said. He then reached into the guy's pocket and retrieved what must have been the guy's phone and headed off in the opposite direction. I stood there and stared into the empty space where he had just been. I couldn't be sure, but it sounded like he just wanted us to off the guy and throw him in a lake, but that was the last option in my mind.

"Ezra!" They all yelled in unison. "Come on!" I snapped out of it and ran to the passenger side of the truck where the front seat was left open for me.

"Where to?" Job asked as I shut the door.

"Let's just take him to the farm and try to fix him up as best we can until we think of something to do," I said.

"Sounds like a plan," Job replied, peeling out of the alley. Neil and Nehemiah banged their fists against the back window, reminding us of our bleeding passenger. We tried to avoid the busy lanes along the Beachside Walk for the most part, doing our best to navigate through the beach neighborhoods and finally making our way across the bridge and blowing onto County Road 1 with record speeds. As we tore smoke trails into the country, I got a text message from June.

"Everything ok?"

What a time to ask, I thought. I texted her back something generic in order to try and throw her off the idea that things were actually extremely wrong.

"Everything's cool. See you later tonight,"

I said, placing my phone back in my pocket as we turned into the farm. It was really late, so Job turned the truck lights off as we idled down the driveway to the barn. We stopped and hopped out, all five of us grabbing onto the stranger and hoisting him out of the truck bed. We carried him into the old feed and tack room, where we knew Moses never went, and laid him down on a bed of hay and horse blankets, rather like Jesus, from what I hear and see on Ma's nativity set. He moaned some more. The huge knife was sticking out of his shoulder; dangerously close to his neck. It looked like this sword called The Demon Slayer that Nehemiah had bought at a garage sale once. It was like something from Masters of the Universe—that sword. I'd never seen so much blood in my life. The closest I'd gotten was a couple months ago when I'd shoved that fellow out of the camper and popped his arm all to hell. It was a miracle this poor guy wasn't dead.

"What do we do?" Job asked as Nehemiah shut the door which immediately re-opened and closed for Neil. "Yeah. Thom just said 'handle it'. I don't know what the hell that means," I growled.

"Well, we need to get the knife out and put pressure on the bleeding. That's obvious," Saul suggested. None of us were doctors, but we knew that much from getting snake bites and getting chop-happy with machetes while growing up on the farm. Honestly, it didn't feel too much like Thom cared if the guy lived or died. He just wanted him out of his hair. I touched the knife gracefully. It was embedded deep and reinforced with several hooked teeth, from what I could tell.

"We could always use that pesticide or mole cricket poison or whatever that stuff was from the day we sprayed Nelson," Saul suggested. "It's sitting right over there."

"No way. We trying to put the guy in a coma?" I asked. "Maybe Rompun?"

"I don't know if Moses has any left," Saul replied. "go check on it," he ordered Neil and Nehemiah. They immediately swung out the door and closed it behind them. "Might be a little strong, don't you think?" Saul asked me.

"Who knows, man? He's a big dude. Guess we'll see," I replied.

"Guys, he's not going to make it much longer," Job started. "It looks like it only went through his muscle. It's got to be close to some important shit, though, and he's lost a ton of blood."

"Yeah, well, we're going to have to stitch him up, too," I added."Ma' teach any of you guys how to sew?" Neil and Nehemiah returned with a needle filled to the brim with horse tranquilizer. "This is all he had left," Nehemiah said. "Hope he doesn't need it anytime soon."

"Give it here. I'll do it," I said, taking the needle in my hand. The guy was in so much pain, all he could do was groan. He hadn't said an actual word the entire time. I took the point and slowly inserted it near the knife blade. I wasn't much for just jabbing needles in people, like you see in war movies or whatever. I was also a little hesitant about using the entire dose, so I only squeezed out a little. "Wait! Shit, was I supposed to put that in his muscle or in his vein?" I asked impatiently.

"Uh … I think you put it in his muscle," Nehemiah said. "The vein seems like it would kill him or something."

"Ok," I breathed. "So I guess we'll just wait a few minutes and rip this thing out." I lightly experimented with several different grips for removing the blade. The brothers and Neil were all gathered around closely. "Someone get some gauze or towels or something," I said. "When I pull this out, it's going to start spilling all over the place." Nehemiah left and quickly returned with a roll of paper towels.

"Would it be best to cauterize it with a hot brand or something?" Neil asked,

"No, dude. I thought we were going to try to sew it!" I replied.

"I left my purse at the motel," Saul added sarcastically. "Who in hell knows how to sew!"

"Actually, the brand's not a bad idea," Job added. "The guy's so out of it, he'll hardly notice. Plus, the knife's going to leave a nasty scar anyway." I sat there blank for a minute and then finally gave in for lack of a better option.

"Alright. Neil, Nehemiah, go heat one up," I ordered. They raced back out the door. I turned to Job and Saul. "... So should I wait for them to get back, or should we do this?"

"Let's just do it," Saul said.

"Yeah, they have weak stomachs anyway," Job added. "They wouldn't want to see it."

"Alright," I replied, gripping the blade tightly. "Here we go." I wasn't about to just give it a gentle tug. This was like ripping a hook out of a bleeding fish. I yanked the knife, and I meant it the first time. The guy screamed like you wouldn't believe. The blade had come clean out. As I observed the thorny edges, covered in blood, Job and Saul held paper towels to his neck to stop up the bleeding and stuffed more into his mouth to muffle the sounds.

Neil and Nehemiah returned with a red-hot electric branding iron in the shape of a cross. I'd seen it before, lying around Moses' "office." We'd never actually branded anything on the farm. It had just always been here. The cross must have been a common motif with the farm's previous owners.

"Aw man! We wanted to see that!" Nehemiah shouted.

"Sorry," I said. "Give me that thing. Actually, do you want to do it?" I asked him.

"Sure," Nehemiah replied. Without a second's notice, Nehemiah stuck the glowing iron cross to the man's neck, sending a burnt blood smoke rising from the wound. The man's eyes opened wide as he screamed even louder and then instantly fainted.

"Well that was easy …" Saul said, looking at Job.

"Why don't you give us a little warning next time," I said, leaning in close to observe the cauterized wound. It looked terrible, but the bleeding had stopped. "Think we need to clean it?" I asked, looking at Saul and Job. We observed the guy laying there still as ever.

"Ah, screw it," Job said. "If he wakes up not dead, he'll be fine."

"I need a cigarette," Saul spoke. We all agreed and got up to exit the room.

"Should someone stay with him?" Neil asked. We all looked back at the sizzling body lying sound asleep or sound dead on a stack of saddle blankets. "Ah hell, man," I said, as Saul opened the door into the barn.

Before we could even all get out of the room, Saul shoved us back, reaching around the doorpost to turn off the light in the feed room.

"What are you doing?" Job barked.

"Shut up!" Saul whispered. "It's Moses." Nehemiah

and Neil immediately ran over and covered knife guy with blankets as I peeked around the door.

"It's ok. He's not coming over here," I whispered. Moses was walking out of the house. His orange ember was guiding the way. Job, Saul and I crawled out of the door and crept low across the clay floor of the barn. It was totally dark. He couldn't see us. We laid there quietly and watched as Moses glided across the moonlit yard and headed for the horse trailer.

"He knows," Job said.

"He must think we're asleep inside," I whispered back. The night was quiet. We could almost hear his footsteps traveling across the grass. He bent down a few times around the wheel wells, squatting twice to look at the tires.

"He can tell it's got something in it," Saul observed.

"Yep," I agreed. Neil and Nehemiah were now crouched at the door.

"What's he doing? Can you see him?" Nehemiah asked. Job raised his head and looked at them, placing a finger over his mouth and then laying back down. Moses was now around the back of the trailer. We heard the lock clanging against the side and then the old chain rattle through the handle as he opened the doors with a squeal. He had seen the barrels. We sat there speechless as Moses slammed the metal doors and stomped off towards the house. He was on his way to wake us. We waited until he had gone inside, then we jumped up, ran into the feed room and shut the door. It was still dark inside.

"Alright. Any minute now, Moses is going to come busting out of that house, and then he's coming straight for the barn. Get him out of here," I said, pointing to the knife guy. "Take him to the old barn. I'll handle Moses."

"You can't take Moses by yourself, Ezra," Job reasoned.

"Yeah. No one can whoop their own dad," Saul added.

"It's alright," I replied. "Just go. Get him out of here. I'll be back there in a little bit."

The brothers and Neil lifted the unconscious slab of meat—each grabbing a limb—and carried him quickly out the door. Moses was now stomping across the yard towards the barn.

Within moments, the brothers had disappeared through the back, and Moses was upon me. He grabbed the collar of my shirt and yanked me like a dog, slamming my body against the barn wall and holding me there. This was tame. He'd done it to all of us. It was where I'd gotten the technique for the fellow at the Winnebago. It's always been Moses' move.

"What the hell is going on?!" he roared.

"Nothing. What the hell is going on with you, man?" I boldly replied, as if the full contact wasn't awkward enough. Moses stood there, puzzled for a second—shrouded in darkness with nothing but his breathing orange ember glow sticking out of his mouth. He lifted it from his lips and held it close to my neck.

"I told you if I found out you guys were trying to make me look stupid to my customers, I'd kill you. Now, explain to me why there are a shitload of Beckins' grease barrels in my trailer." I pulled away from the ember as much as I could, but it followed me wherever I went.

"Yeah, the asshole's like half a year behind on his payments. We told him he owed you a whole mess of grease if he couldn't pay." I breathed. Moses growled. "Hey, at least you're getting something …" I added. Moses looked at me strong and silent. We remained there for a moment, locked in an almost endless curiosity. Moses flicked his cigarette to the clay floor and crushed the butt beneath a twist of his leg, never taking his eyes off me.

"… Just as well …" he started. A questioning expression came over my face as he released me, looking away and pulling another cigarette from its home in his shirt pocket. "I was coming out to shoot that sunovabitch's horse tonight when I saw the trailer sitting low." Moses touched his pockets.

"Here," I said, extending my lighter to his mouth. He turned and sucked the ember to life. I put the lighter back into my pocket and fluffed my shirt a bit.

"Sorry about that," he said, pointing at the wall and taking another drag. It was the first time he'd ever said it to me.

"It's alright," I replied. It really wasn't alright, but the awkwardness had to be over.

"Where are the dumbasses?" he asked almost playfully as he stared off into the night.

"No idea," I replied.

"What are you doing out here?"

"I just got home," I answered hastily. "I was on the phone."

"Mm …" Moses grunted. "I'm going back inside," he said, throwing his cigarette down and beginning to walk off. "… you know your momma has a tattoo of a black guy on her ass?" he asked, looking back at me.

"… I … did not know that," I replied quietly. With that, Moses disappeared into the moonlight over the yard. I stood there until he cleared the front door and then made my way around the rear of the barn.

The old barn was a tired-looking place. It was an external group of stalls connected at the backs of each other beneath one shared roof. On the far end was an old hay storage and the entrance to Moses' cellar. I walked quickly down the front of the stalls, looking into each one for a sign of my brothers, but they were nowhere to be found. Once I'd reached the end, I immediately heard a voice at my feet and jumped for dear life.

"Ezra!" it spoke in a harsh whisper. "Down here!" I saw now that I was standing next to that cellar. Its flat door creaked open every time words came out—giving the appearance that the cellar itself was beckoning me. I could hear whispers and see light flickering inside. I bent down.

"Are you guys all in there?!" I asked.

"Yeah. Get in, quick." the door replied. It was Saul's voice. The cellar opened its mouth wide. Saul stood holding the hatch open, scouring the landscape for spies like some WWII tank soldier. I could see flashlights waving around way down at the bottom of the step ladder.

"Dude, this thing is bigger than I thought!" I marveled.

"That's what she said," Saul replied comically. I ignored him. "Get in. You've got to see this," he added. Someone shined a light as I searched for the first rung of the stepladder. It was just like you'd imagine, creaky and unstable. I pulled the door closed and felt my way down backwards, taking one step slowly after the next. It smelled the way dirt smells on your hands or tastes in your mouth. There was something warm and soothing about it that reminded me of being younger. The lights bounced around the room. I could see and hear now that it was bigger than I'd always imagined it to be. I was immediately reminded of my dream. The look and feel didn't appear to be much different apart from the size. As I reached the dirt floor, Job handed me a flashlight that was already shining.

"Here, take this," he said, shining his into my face.

"Thanks," I said, slapping it out of his hand. "Get that thing out of my face, douche."

"Ass," he replied, retrieving it from the ground.

"Where did you guys get all these?" I asked, puzzled.

"Moses must keep forgetting and bringing more of them down here," Saul said. Nehemiah and Neil were several feet away, observing some large piece of machinery. It must have been what Moses was mending. I started to shine my light on it when I heard a moan coming from near one of the support beams. I aimed my light at our guest who I'd almost forgotten was there.

"Yeah, he's awake, by the way," Saul said. I went over and bent down next to the poor guy as my brothers and Neil were now all surrounding the great, mammoth piece of equipment. I could hear them arguing quietly amongst themselves as I tried to get knife guy to say something.

"Hey, man. How are you feeling?" I asked. He looked at me like he'd just heard the dumbest question of all time.

"Bad ..." he replied. "I need some water."

"I don't have any water right now, man. We've got to hide out here for a bit—"

"WATER!" Neil yelled. "There's water down there!" I shined my light at the brothers. They were all circling the complicated, iron colossus in the middle of the cellar, pointing their own lights deep into its recesses. I could tell now that it was a pump of some kind.

"I think this is an old well or something," Saul observed. I walked over to take a look for myself, forgetting about the guy on the floor for just a minute.

"This thing is old, man …" I said. "I wonder if he's fixed it yet."

"Who?" Nehemiah asked.

"Moses," I answered.

"This is obviously what he's been greasing up," Job added.

"Right," Nehemiah said. We scoured the machine for an "on" switch. It was a rusted collage of cogs and pistons about the size of a Volks Wagon. None of us had a clue how to turn the thing on.

"I think this is a lever," someone said as the large contraption immediately began moving and firing loudly. Five beams bounced to the rear of the machine. It was knife guy. He was up and leaning on the lever, rattling along with the massive, moving pump. We watched curiously from one side as he searched the base of the machine. "ANYONE HAVE A CUP?!" he yelled. We looked at each other and then back at him without a word. He mouthed something I couldn't hear above the growling and shaking of the pump. He then bent down behind the machine where a set of large copper pipes ran up the block wall of the cellar. With hands cupped, he began collecting water from a leak at the base of the pipes.

"THAT WATER IS PROBABLY DIRTY, MAN …" Nehemiah yelled. Knife guy didn't acknowledge anyone—just kept on drinking, taking handfuls and splashing them on his wound to clean it. When he'd had his fill, he walked over and threw the lever back. The motor in the machine squealed loudly, shook abruptly and then hissed until completely still and quiet. "That water is probably dirty, man ..." Nehemiah repeated verbatim.

"It's better than no water," the guy said, touching his wound gently, grimacing. "Where are we?"

"We work for this chick who owns that motel you got stabbed at," I started. "Well, I don't know if she owns it—"

"—and we're not officially employed by her," Job interrupted and then whispered in my ear, "he's a cop, dude."

"Anyway, we're on our farm ... hiding," I added.

"I can't feel my left side," said knife guy. "Can someone give me a ride to the hospital?" We all stood still and silent. Knife guy looked up from his blood-soaked shirt. "... I'm not looking to turn anyone in. I get it." We kept quiet. Knife guy laughed a little and immediately winced. "Guys, seriously, no worries.... I appreciate your help." He moved over and sat down on the ladder. "I'm just in a lot of pain." I turned around and faced Job and Saul. I spoke to them in a low voice as they came in close.

"We need to get him to River Medical or something."

"No way, dude!" Job growled.

"He needs attention," I said.

"I don't know, Ezra," Saul started. "We could get in trouble."

"Right, and we won't get in trouble if we detain a police officer ..." I replied. "Besides, the dude's going to get Gangrene or AIDS or something if he doesn't get looked at soon."

"Guys!" came a shout from the steps. Our heads snapped to the ladder. "Please ..." knife guy said. I looked back at Job and Saul.

"We're still following my lead, remember?" I walked over and grabbed him under his left shoulder.

"What about what Thom said?" Saul asked.

"Doesn't matter." I replied. "Do you see Thom here dealing with this? Someone get his other arm." Nehemiah rushed over and lifted from the other side. "I need someone to go up there and open the door. And check to make sure it's all clear." Neil mounted the stepladder with a smaller light in his mouth and was at the top in seconds. As he cracked the hatch open, we could see morning light coming in. It was faint, but it was definitely sunlight. "Just give him a second," I said. We don't want to run into Moses. He'll be up soon."

"Who's Moses?" knife guy grunted.

"Our dad," Nehemiah said.

"What's your name?" I asked.

"Blake," knife guy answered.

"Blake, we'll have you out of here in a minute," I said as Neil lifted the hatch and shined back down at us, motioning for us to come up. "Alright, coast is clear. You ready, Blake?"

"Yeah," he said, as Nehemiah and I helped him up the first set of steps. In the blue morning light, I noticed the wound on his neck had changed. It appeared to be smaller, but it could have just been the remaining shadows playing tricks on me. The wooden stepladder was almost wide enough for the three of us. Nehemiah and I took turns losing our footing on either side, but soon, we had reached the top. Neil held the door open as we spilled out onto the ground and laid low. The ground was freshly wet. Job and Saul made their way out, closed the door and came to lay beside us—all with flashlights still in-hand. There was no use in leaving them inside or pretending we hadn't been there. Moses would know regardless.

We could see the house through the wooden fences that surrounded the large paddock next to the barn. There was no sign of Moses yet. He should've been getting up, by the look things. He was usually heading out to the barn at this time of the morning. It must have been about six.

"Alright," I said, loud enough for everyone to hear me, "when I get up, let's make a run for the back of the barn." The brothers, Neil and Blake agreed with various nods and looks. "… One, two, three …" We all leapt up and hoofed it the twenty yards to the rear side of the barn. I thought for a second that I caught a flash of Blake's neck looking awfully ordinary. We came to a stop and crouched down single file. I peered through a crack in the wooden siding at the back of the barn to see if I could catch a glimpse of Moses. Still no sign of him. I turned around to get another look at Blake's neck when I was met with something I didn't expect.

"Woah, dude! Easy!" I said, staring down the barrel of Blake's Beretta that we must have conveniently neglected to see on his ankle or in his underwear or wherever. It took my brothers and Neil a second to catch on to what was happening.

"Slowly stand," Blake ordered. "Everyone else get back." I instinctively put my hands up as my brothers and Neil slowly stood and backed up. "Put your hands down, dumbass."

"Ooh, snappy," I remarked, lowering my hands. He was alternating looks between me and them. He didn't trust my brothers. I wouldn't either.

"Way back," he ordered them, attempting to put as much distance between he and them as he possibly could. He then grabbed onto the back of my shirt and brought the gun to my jaw. I don't know what he was planning on doing—maybe blowing my mouth off?

"So I guess you're calling for back up?" I asked. "Bringing us in ..."

"No," he replied. "My phone's conveniently missing," he said, feeling his pockets with his free hand. He had situated us nicely. I was now standing between him and the guys. We were close to the rear barn doorway. They were huddled close to the cellar. "Do you have your phone on you?" he asked calmly.

"Yeah," I replied. "What's the number to the station, 911?" I retrieved my phone from my pocket and held it up for him to grab.

"No, not me," he said. "You're going to call him."

"Who?" I asked.

"I think you guys called him Thom?" Blake added. I dropped my arm.

"Why do you want to call Thom?" I questioned. My brother's and Neil wore confused expressions like my own.

"Dial!" he demanded.

"It's actually an iPhone," I remarked, "so I'll just think about him and the call will go through."

"Why are you being such a smartass?" Blake asked. "BACK!" He shouted at Job and Saul who had made some slow ground toward us.

"It's what I do when I'm being threatened," I stated. "Self-defense mechanism, I suppose. I'm like a sarcastic ... animal or ... something. I'm a sar-cat-fish ..." The phone was ringing.

"Put it on speaker," Blake ordered.

"Way ahead of you, man," I said, holding the phone for all to hear as it continued to ring.

"Hey, duder," the device spoke.

"Hey, Thom," I started. "Listen, we've got a bit of a situation here—"

"No shit ..." he interjected. "Please tell me you guys got some sleep. It's early, man."

"Dude, what planet are you on?" I said angrily. "Of course we didn't get any sleep. I'm being held at gunpoint right now, you cock."

"... What?" the phone said in a muffled voice.

"It's Blake, this cop who's life we saved ..." I said, glancing back at my captor. "He's pissed about something."

"Why are you calling me if he has you at gunpoint?" Thom asked.

"Your guess is as good as mine," I said. "I'm going to keep shooting the shit with you until he gives me some instructions, though. How's your mom—" Blake snatched the phone out of my hand and spoke into it like it was a walkie-talkie.

"Hey, Thom," he said.

"Hello," the phone answered back.

"I bet you don't know this, but you actually have a few things of mine that need to be returned," Blake stated.

"You're right," Thom answered. "I didn't know that."

"Yeah, nothing much, just a few girls you took out of my house," he said, shaking and sweating the way any crazed hostage-taker does when revealing a dark secret.

177

"… So, you're not a cop?" Thom asked.

"I'm a collector," Blake replied. "It seems you guys have been tapping my resources for quite some time now."

"I'm having a hard time putting a name with a face here, Blake …" Thom said. Blake shook me and spoke violently into the phone,

"Do you think you can just go into someone's house anytime you want and take their property?! If something's chained to the wall, it's meant to stay there!" I had no idea what he was talking about, but Thom seemed to be getting the idea.

"Oh, right … so you're him," Thom said. "Bravo on the cover job, man. No one would expect a police officer to keep malnourished rape toys chained up like dogs at his marina-side cottage."

"Yeah, man," I added, "except—oh wait—it's 2010 and that's exactly what I'd expect …" Blake shoved and jerked violently on my shirt, digging his gun deeper into my cheek.

"I want you here. Right now," Blake demanded.

"Ok… Ok… Look, it's no problem," Thom said, clearly trying his best to soothe the situation. "Just calm down. Do you need me to bring anything?"

"You owe me a skinny blonde bitch and possibly a brunette one if she's come back looking for me …" he answered.

"Well, now Blake, the brunette did come by just before you called. Some gypsy-looking chick named Zordon or something," Thom said. "She and Kristy ran off in her car. I think they're looking for you. You'd better hope Kristy hasn't spilled the beans, brother."

"Get here and be alone, or I will shoot someone in the head," Blake said firmly. "I promise." He ended the call and tossed my phone into a pile of horse turd on the side of the barn. "Let's move." Blake shoved me into the barn. The brothers and Neil followed at a distance. "That's it. Not too close!" he yelled back to them. I just knew that any minute Moses was going to come rounding the front corner of the barn and all hell would go down.

"Where are we going?" I asked as we walked backwards between the long rows of stalls and towards the front yard. He didn't answer. He didn't know. He was focused on my brothers and Neil.

"What time is it?" he asked.

"You threw my phone in the shit ..." I answered stoically.

"WHAT TIME IS IT?" he yelled to the guys. They felt their pockets. None of them even owned cell phones, but Nehemiah wore a watch.

"6:37," He called out.

"How long of a drive is it from the motel to here?" he asked me. I lied.

"... Maybe ten minutes."

"Where's a good place to hide?" he asked.

"... Well, the cellar was pretty prime," I answered.

"—No, not the cellar," Blake interjected. "I need some place where I can see."

"There's the office," I suggested—half wanting Moses to discover us now. What better place than his office where he drank his morning cup of cigarettes ...

I led Blake to the door. He threw it wide-open and stood by as each of my brothers and Neil filed into the tiny room. It was nothing special—just a concrete floor, a wall of empty shelves and an aluminum desk with a bunch of crap on it. There was an inch of dust on everything. Ma' Cotton called it the Moon Room. When we were all inside, Blake backed out and closed the door.

"Why didn't you guys bum rush him?!" I asked angrily.

"Because he would have shot you in the face," Saul answered. I straightened my shirt out.

"Well, I still think one of you could have run off and gotten help or something," I replied.

"Look, it doesn't matter," Job said. "Moses keeps a 12-gauge in here somewhere. Everyone look around for it." I gave it about ten seconds before I gave up and went to the window that faced the driveway. Everyone else was still poking around.

"Wonder where Moses is," I said. "He's usually out here by now. His truck's still here."

"Damn, where is that thing?!" Job demanded, slamming his fist on the desk.

"Hold up," I said. "There's a black car pulling into the driveway. Anyone recognize it?" The brothers and Neil rushed to the window.

"Never seen it before," said Nehemiah.

"Nope," agreed Saul.

"It's got to be the girls," I stated. Blake was now walking casually towards the car from the barn. I could see his neck plainly. Not a scratch. In the distance, a blonde girl and a brunette were stepping out of the black car which was now parked at the edge of the driveway by the road. At first sight of Blake, the blonde ran around the side of the car and grabbed the brunette, attempting to hold her back, but she yanked free. She was now walking full-speed towards Blake. The blonde was yelling something. We could hear it faintly, but not enough to tell what she was saying. She obviously didn't want the brunette going anywhere near Blake.

When Blake and the brunette finally met in the middle of the driveway, they hugged and then kissed.

"This girl has obviously been misinformed," I observed.

"Or that dark hair is a sign of her devious nature, and she's with him," Neil suggested.

"I didn't even know you knew what that meant," said Saul.

"What, 'dark?'" Neil asked.

"Idiot ..." I said.

"Bet you a million dollars he pulls the gun on her," said Saul.

"Bet you're right," I agreed. We watched then as the inevitable happened like clockwork; like we'd seen it a hundred times in a movie, Blake reached for his back, pulled the gun and grabbed the brunette around the neck with his arm.

"Wow, you really called it," Nehemiah said.

"Wait!" Neil exclaimed. "Who's that?" Two male figures were coming up the driveway.

"It's Thom," I answered, "and that's John on the right."

"Did they walk?" Job asked. "Where's their car?"

"Probably parked it on the road," I replied. Soon, Blake had spotted both of them and positioned the brunette between he and them. He was good at that move. John spotted the blonde standing alone by the car and ran over. They hugged, he spoke something to her and then he helped her into the car. He then joined Thom and they began walking toward Blake and his unsuspecting hostage.

"I say we go out now while his attention is on them," Job suggested.

"Yep," I agreed. "The more pressure we put on him; the sooner he'll trip up."

"What if he shoots her?" Nehemiah asked.

"He won't shoot her," Saul replied. "He's got no where to go after that. He'll have lost all his leverage. He knows that."

The brothers and Neil let me lead the way. I opened the door and immediately heard the loud communication happening between Thom, John and Blake.

"I want you to take me to your boss!" Blake yelled. "That woman!" We slowly stepped out into the sunlight, making our way towards the driveway. Maybe I could sneak up behind him and tackle him to the ground, I thought. By chance, I quickly glanced at the house and saw Moses standing behind the glass door on the front of the house. He was watching me move slowly towards Blake. He shook his head, warning me not to do what I was thinking of doing. The brothers and Neil were several feet behind me. They hadn't noticed Moses yet.

Before I could take another step, Blake quickly turned to us, yanking the brunette along.

"HOLD IT!" he yelled, pointing the gun at all of us. "Get back in the room."

"No," I challenged him. No reply … not with words, at least. He aimed his gun at my feet and shot the ground by my toes. "Get on that side!" he demanded, motioning towards Thom and John with the gun. That was enough for me. I led the guys around toward Thom and John and the blonde who was still sitting in the car, looking on at the situation.

"Listen, man," Thom started, "this obviously isn't going anywhere. What's going to make this better?"

"I already told you," Blake said, "I want to see her."

"Fine," Thom replied. "Let's go. Get in the car with us, and we'll take you to the motel, but I'm just telling you, this is a stupid move on your part."

"Where's the car?" Blake asked.

"It's parked down on the road," Thom answered, "but we've got something we need to drop off here first." Thom whispered something into John's ear who then quickly jogged off towards the road.

"Fine. Let's go," Blake said, yanking once more on the brunette's neck. She was looking bad. Her hair was like a mop in her face which was soaking wet. She could have been dead for all I knew.

"Ezra," Thom spoke as Blake began walking over.

"What's up," I replied. He motioned for me to come closer and waited until Blake had passed him with the brunette and gone down to the road.

"We're bringing you a guy right now who was involved in the incident last night. I need you to keep him just for a while."

"Who is the girl?" I asked.

"Her name is Zwinny," Thom stated. "Not exactly sure how she's connected. We just know he was planning the same thing for her as he did with Kristy."

"The blonde ..." I said, looking at the tented car windows.

"Right," Thom answered. "Her and like a million other girls we've ganked from his place. Needless to say, he's pissed."

"... Dude, you could stop this if you wanted," I said abstractly.

"I do want to stop it, Ezra," Thom replied., "but unfortunately, I can't foresee every time someone's going to develop a vendetta against us."

"No," I started, "I mean stop all of this. You could put an end to the entire situation; the motel, the oil … even B." Thom looked at me curiously for a second, and then I saw it click in his eyes. He looked down, shaking his head.

"I don't have that kind of power," he said. "B's going to keep going and going as long as she gets to watch the whole thing unfold behind glass. We're all just pieces—minutemen, called at the drop of a hat to fix the messes. Believe me, I'd stop it if I could. We've all had this affect us in one way or another. The extra wedding ring that John wears on his pinky belongs to the girl in the car. I can't explain how that makes me feel. It's just the nature of the beast." He gave a half-sincere smile and turned around as he headed down to the road. "We'll be right back."

When I turned around in frustration, Moses was strolling casually towards me from the house. The brothers and Neil had begun to walk over as well, but Moses gave them the signal to stay put. I figured this would start with a hand to the neck like it usually did. Surprisingly, when he arrived in front of me, he had his hands in his pockets. He was watching the blonde pull out of the driveway in the brunette's car.

"I don't want to know what's going on," he said. "It looks like it's leaving, whatever it is." I looked back towards the road and then returned to Moses.

"It is leaving," I said.

"You know, when you were kids, you were always going and getting yourselves into something," Moses started. He reached in his shirt pocket and half pulled a cigarette out before pausing and pushing it back down. He looked upwards. "… and now, you're grown men, and you've found all new ways to bring hell down on your heads."

"Moses, I didn—"

"My brother died trying to save my life," Moses interjected. I never even knew he had a brother. I was suddenly on the heels of his every word. "That's blood you can't go and find and pay for." He was looking far away—farther than I'd ever dared to look. "It's tragedy," he continued, "that all you can do—with that same blood—is die trying to end theirs." He looked back at the brothers and Neil. I was floored. My convictions had been completely misunderstood and reduced to mere mischief. I opened my mouth once again to speak, but the words were stolen from me. "You don't understand it. You'll face death head-on, and you'll be alone."

With that, Moses walked off towards the barn. The cigarette finally made it to his mouth, and I saw smoke rising from under the bill of his hat as he went off to work. The brothers and Neil finally approached.

"What was that all about?" asked Saul with utmost curiosity.

"Nothing …" I replied.

"Nothing? What did he say?" Job demanded.

"… Said we better wrap this thing up," I answered. Thom and John were now coming back up the driveway with a third dude who wore a pillowcase on his head. "We've got one last babysitting job first," I said. "Take him around back—the long way. Get him somewhere where Moses won't see him."

"Who is he?" Nehemiah asked. I ignored him.

"And while you're back there," I started, "get the cellar cleaned as close to how you found it as possible. No reason to get Moses even more pissed than he already is." Thom and John reached us with the pillowcase kid and handed him off to the brothers and Neil. "Don't let him see you," I said as they marched off.

"His name is Nate," Thom said as I turned to face him. "There was a mix up last night and he got knocked out. He wakes up this morning and comes asking questions. He remembers a lot more than we thought he would."

"So, what, is he the witness to a crime or something?" I asked.

"No," John spoke up. "He's in the way."

"He's just baggage we picked up," Thom added. "We'll be back to pick him up either late tonight or in the morning. Just have to clear some things up first."

"Thom … we're done after this," I said. He looked at me and breathed a deep breath.

"… Fair enough," he replied. "Back later," he said as he and John walked off towards the road one last time. I stood there for a moment before turning to face the farm. It was about time I called June. The one problem therein was that my phone was lying somewhere in a manure pile. I needed to check with my brothers and Neil first to make sure everything was ok. We were almost there. Hold on, June.

As I rounded the back corner of the barn, I did a quick scan of where Blake had thrown my phone, but saw nothing, so I kept moving. I discovered the brothers hunched down near the middle of the old barn where Moses had converted the middle stall into a storage room. Neil shouted the second he noticed me approaching.

"Ezra, come here! Quick!" he yelled. I ran to the door and saw the pillowcase kid sitting propped up against the wall, unconscious next to a canister of that old mole cricket poison.

"We told him to stay away from it!" Nehemiah exclaimed. "Neil warned him it would put him in a coma if he sprayed it. Next thing you know, he's got the damned thing sticking straight into his nose! He gave it one good pump and before we could get to him, he was out …" I ran into the room and tried to feel for a pulse on the kid's wrist. Nothing.

"Come on, big guy!" I said, slapping the kid across his face several times. "Why didn't you guys just take it out of here?" I asked, feeling again for a pulse. This time, I could feel something faint, but it wasn't much.

"I don't know!" Nehemiah replied. Job and Saul entered the room. "Did Nelson make it?!" I asked quickly.

"What? Nelson who?" Saul asked.

"Nelson, the pig! The pig, Nelson! Did he live?!" I yelled. Saul rushed out of the room as Job and Neil bent down next to me.

"Is he alive right now?" Job asked.

"Barely," I said. "Help me lay him down flat. He needs to be on his back." We stretched him out on the dirty floor. "Why the hell would somebody poison themselves?" I asked. We stood up slowly, clapping the dust off of our shirts.

"Maybe he wants to kill himself," Job suggested. Neil left and quickly returned with one of the horse's water buckets. He tossed it on the kid, drenching him from head to toe, but nothing happened.

"Alright, no more from you," I said, shoving Neil out of the room. Saul came running back up.

"Nelson's fine," he said. "Looks completely normal. He should be fine, too, within a couple … days or something. Just need to let the stuff run its course."

"Shit," I said, breathing heavy. I wiped the sweat off my face with my sleeve and sat down on a bucket, trying to recover. "Man, when is this going to end?!" I growled, laying back against the wall. The brothers left the room and went and joined Neil outside. I closed my eyes for just a minute. I was instantly and uncontrollably drawn to sleep as the voices around me and in my head slowly died. I slept. I slept so hard that weight left my body. I didn't move. Period.

When I awoke, it felt like Rip Van Winkle. I opened my eyes and my right arm was covered in drool. My mouth was open, and I couldn't feel my limbs. That's when you know you slept. I wiped the drool off my arm onto my jeans and then wiped the corners of my mouth with my sleeve. I immediately noticed the space on the floor where the pillowcase kid had been was now empty. My jaw hit the floor. It was that feeling of waking up and realizing life's been going on without you. I walked to the door and looked out. There was no sign of anyone. It had maybe been an hour. Before I knew it, I noticed the brothers and Neil rounding the corner with the pillowcase kid. Nehemiah and Neil were holding onto his arms. He was awake, and he looked exhausted.

"We were having a smoke," Job said.

"Oh, weird …" I interrupted sarcastically.

"… We were having a smoke and we see him haul ass out of the room and make a break for the house," Job went on. "He's been saying weird stuff, man." The pillowcase kid was shaking wildly. His eyes were bulging out of his head, and he was sweating bullets.

"How long was I out?" he asked.

"About an hour," Saul said. "Why would you do something like that?"

"I had to know …" he mumbled.

"Hey," I started, "Nate, right?" He shook his head, looking down. "Why'd you poison yourself. You could have died, you know …" Neil and Nehemiah slowly released his arms as he sat down on a cinder block.

"No one was going to tell me," he said, half talking to himself. "I needed to know what to do next. I needed to ask her."

"Ask who what, Nate?" I tried to understand.

"Dee," he said. I looked back at the brothers.

"Who is Dee?" I asked.

"Some girl who tells me what to do," he answered. "They went to the motel to see B, but she was gone. They're going to the club to find her. We have to go now."

"How could you possibly know that?" Job asked.

"We have to go now!" Nate repeated.

"Why?" I questioned. "What's going to happen?

"If we don't go, good people are going to die," he insisted.

"People have already died," Saul replied. Nate looked up at us in earnest. At once, I could tell he had instantly regained his sanity, and I believed him.

"It's all of us," he started. "If we don't get over there now, we'll have lost our chance to end this." We all stood there for a moment, looking at each other. "… Where's the car?" he asked.

After a collaborative call/search in the piles near the barn, my phone was discovered and we were in the truck and on our way to Fran's within ten minutes. I sent June a quick text to make sure she still loved me.

"Love you, too. Call me later. Can't wait to hear how the Cotton Bros. Crime Syndicate is going,"

she texted back. I could never tell over text if she was joking or not. I didn't contact anyone else. Thom would have told us to stay put. I wasn't listening to Thom anymore. I was interested in seeing if Nate's visions were giving him instructions that were worth a damn. He and I were the only ones in the cab. The brothers and Neil had removed the last oil barrel and were riding in the bed of the truck. I think they were afraid of him.

"So, what were you doing at the motel?" I asked. he kept his head straight forward.

"I was spying on Zwinny's new boyfriend," he answered.

"Zwinny is the brunnette ..." I said.

"Right," he replied. "And her boyfriend's name is Blake."

"Well, whatever suspicions you had about him were right—" I began.

"I know," Nate interjected. I looked over at him and then back at the road. We listened to the truck working beneath us. "I'm confused about what I did," he said.

"How do you mean?" I asked.

"I had suspicions, yes," he began, "but did that give me the right to try to mess it up?"

"It sure as hell did," I replied. "That guy had sick plans for her, man. You're going to be glad you did it one day. Who knows where she'd be right now if it weren't for you."

"Yeah, but I didn't have grounds," he said. "It was only jealousy. Besides, where is Zwinny now? She's still at the mercy of his appetite, and I'm still chasing her." I looked over at him again and then back at the road. He had a good point, but I can't say I wouldn't have done the same thing having been put in his shoes.

"There they are," I said as we pulled into No Hands Fran's. The green Rubicon was parked in front of the door, but there were no other cars to be seen. Blake was still holding Zwinny against him with the gun to her head, and Thom and John were standing next to the Jeep. They didn't look surprised to see us, but I could tell Blake had been pushed to the edge. As we came to a stop, I felt the truck bed rise about a foot as the brothers and Neil hopped out of the back. Nate and I stepped out of the truck and slammed the doors shut. We stood there quietly and watched for a moment as Blake faced back towards Thom and John.

"WHERE IS SHE?!" he yelled. "You said if she wasn't at the motel, she'd be here!"

"Well, it looks like you got what you wanted then," Thom replied. "It's done."

"No," Blake said. "It's not done. I told you; property was stolen from me, and someone's going to pay for it!" With that, Blake pulled the gun from Zwinny's head and aimed it at the closest person, which happened to be Nehemiah. He fired two shots, and Nehemiah went down. We shuddered at first and then collapsed to his side. Job held his head up as Saul and I put pressure on the wound. Only one bullet had hit him—just below the heart.

"There's blood on the ground," Neil observed.

"The bullet must have gone straight through," Nate added. Job took his shirt off, holding Nehemiah's head up with his knees and sliding the shirt underneath his rib cage. His eyes shut tight, but he was writhing from the pain, which was good.

"STAND HIM UP!" Blake screamed, aiming the gun at me. I stood in front of Nehemiah, and the reckless adrenaline immediately kicked in.

"Shoot me, dickhead!" My forwardness seemed to disarm him, the way it did at the farm. He lowered the gun to his side and looked at me in disbelief. "I know," I added with synthetic sympathy, "M9s are heavy.... Hard to lift two-and-a-half pounds unless you're looking at yourself in the bathroom mirror, isn't it?" I said. "Go ahead, aim for my face; maybe you'll hit my balls." He lifted the gun once more and aimed between my eyes. I stood resolute before my brothers, ready to die for them.

Just then, there was crackling in the gravel parking lot, and we turned to see a brown striped truck pulling in. I couldn't believe my eyes, and by the looks of the faces on my brothers and Neil, they couldn't either. It was Moses. He had followed us from the farm.

"What the hell ...?" Job said under his breath. Everyone in the parking lot had their attention set on the truck which had stopped with the driver-side door facing in. We watched for movement through the low tent. He had bent over in his seat and was reaching for something. We all stood silently. The door then unlatched and opened. Moses climbed down out of the truck, and with him came the 12-gauge we had been looking for earlier. In one smooth motion, Moses closed the door, swung the shotgun up into his shoulder, aimed at Blake's head and pulled the trigger. He didn't hesitate. He didn't falter. It must've been a slug, because Zwinny's head was still attached. She fell to her hands and knees, sobbing loudly; the side of her face covered in spatter. Nate quickly ran to her. The rest of us stood in complete shock.

Moses lowered the gun and carefully leaned it up against the side of the truck. He walked over to us and scooped up Nehemiah the way you see Olympic weight lifters clear 200lb barbels with formulaic motions.

"Get the tailgate for me," he said to me. I jumped to the back of the truck and lowered the gate. Moses set Nehemiah in the bed as I hopped up and situated Job's shirt beneath him.

"That's what that dicktard gets ..." Nehemiah smirked. I smiled and then climbed off, shutting the tailgate behind me. Moses placed the gun in the passenger seat and turned to me before getting in.

"He'll be alright," he said.

"Good ..." I replied. Moses climbed into the truck.

"I saw what you did," he said. "... I was wrong." I looked into Moses' eyes for an instant and then backed off as the truck door squealed shut. Within seconds, the truck left the parking lot of Fran's in a white dust cloud towards County Road 1. When I looked back, Job, Saul and Neil were sitting on the hood of the truck, Nate was helping Zwinny into the Jeep, and Thom and John were coming back around from the side of the building after moving what was left of Blake. We met near our truck.

"Who was that?" Thom asked.

"Our dad," I answered, wiping what I could of the blood off on my jeans.

"Your dad is a badass ..." Thom replied. He and John stared off into the distance where the dust cloud had begun to clear up.

"So what happened?" I asked. "What happened to B?" Thom and John looked at each other and then in different directions.

"We don't know," said Thom. "When we got to the motel, her RV was just gone."

"What about the girls?" I asked.

"Gone," John said. "The place was locked up; not a soul to be found." I looked back at Saul and Job and Neil to see if they were hearing this. They all had cigarettes in the corners of their mouths.

"So we came here, thinking she might have come back," Thom added, "but the place was completely zipped. No sign."

"Feels good to be informed …" John spat on the ground. I bit the inside of my lip, shaking my head in amazement.

"What is it?" Thom asked.

"… Ah, it's just … Nate" I said, observing he and Zwinny sitting inside the Jeep together. "He had a sort of dream where he claimed he met a girl who told him you guys would be here."

"He has no clue this place is connected," Thom replied. "How could he possibly know to bring you here?"

"That's exactly what I'm saying!" I explained, "The girl told him to come here!"

"What girl?" John asked.

"I don't know," I answered. "Some girl; a girl named Dee." John shook his head.

"Never heard of her," he said. "But hey, he was right … or she was right, whatever way you want to look at it. Thanks, Dee," he said comically, walking over to join my brothers. I turned back toward Thom who now had a grave expression on his face.

"Thom …?" I repeated. He was just standing there like he'd pissed his pants. "Thom … what the hell is your problem, son?"

"Are you sure her name was Dee?" he asked stoically. I leaned over and shouted in the direction of the Jeep.

"Nate! You did say the girl's name was Dee, right? From the dream?" Nate leaned his head out of the door.

"Yeah. Dee." he replied and leaned back in.

"Why?" I asked. "Do you know a Dee?" No answer. He just stared. "Thom …"

"That's Combs," he finally said.

"What?" I asked, looking intently at him.

"That's Combs," Thom repeated, finally snapping out of it. "B's courier," he said, walking over to a car that was crunching the gravel once again. It was an old man car carrying a scrawny guy with glasses. We all grouped up and walked over. I quickly pulled out my phone to shoot June a text.

We're done :)

I wrote.

Yay.

she replied anticlimactically, followed by a

:)

When the scrawny driver got out of the car, he approached Thom and John who were standing together. He extended an envelope with his right hand.

"Who gets it?" he asked plainly.

"I do," Thom said.

"He does," John added. Thom received the envelope and the three of them stood there for a moment, awkwardly staring at each other until the scrawny guy noticed me, Job, Saul and Neil standing on the other side.

"Are they the farmers?" he asked. Thom and John looked over their shoulders at us and nodded. "Hm," he observed. He then circled back around his open door, got in the old man car and pulled away. We watched him leave and then turned our attention toward Thom who was now opening the envelope. It was a single piece of paper folded thrice with about a paragraph of script scribbled on it. We stood there silently as he finished reading it. He then handed the note to John who read it slower. When he had finished, he and Thom looked at each other, half smiling out of what seemed like utter disbelief.

"Well guys," Thom finally said, "it was nice knowing you." Confusion abounded.

"Yeah," John added. "Remind each other to never do this again." With that, the two of them walked back over to the green Rubicon, got in and pulled away. White dust once again filled the empty parking lot. I looked down to find the tri-folded piece of paper laying gently on the gravel. I bent down and picked it up, reading it aloud as I stood:

Thom, John, Ezra and Nate,

    I've decided it's time to head out, boys. I'm packing up my whole hooker flea circus and following the oil. Combs is selling Fran's, and I don't expect I'll be back. I'd ask you to come along, but I like to recruit regionally. Thom, we had old mop-head disposed of. No worries. And I've got squirt with me. He's happy to be around all these boobies (P.S. I'm sorry I never got to give you that lap dance). John, Bobbie's staying for school—says she's taking a break from the 'profession' for a while (between you and me, I think you can talk her into becoming a decent, monogamous lay). Ezra, I've never in my life seen a family member as loyal as you. Do yourself a favor, though, and kill your brothers and that gay kid you guys hang out with. Nate, sorry you had to sleep with a corpse. Thanks for all your help, guys. Let's do it again sometime!

                    —B

Thank You...

To Dan & Kristi Chaplik and all the Kickstarters for your generous support.

To my family and friends for helping me gauge how far is too far.

To my sweet Kayla, for whom my words live and breathe.

To God, by whom I live and breathe.

Nick May is the twenty-something native Floridian author behind the southern religion deconstruction apparatus known as *MEGABELT*. He earned his B.A. in English and Creative Writing from the University of West Florida and resides in Panama City, Florida where he hosts a monthly open-mic night for writers. Visit Nick's blog at songofsalmon.com, find him on Facebook at facebook.com/authornickmay or follow him on Twitter @heynickmay.

CPSIA information can be obtained at www.ICGtesting.com
Printed in the USA
LVOW080928071011

249521LV00005BA/1/P